Chase Us

Chase Us

SEAN ENNIS

New Harvest • Houghton Mifflin Harcourt

BOSTON   NEW YORK   2014

This edition published by special arrangement with Amazon Publishing

Amazon and the Amazon logo are trademarks of Amazon.com, Inc. or its affiliates.

For information about permission to reproduce selections from this book,
go to www.apub.com.

www.hmhco.com

Library of Congress Cataloging-in-Publication Data
Ennis, Sean, date.
[Stories. Selections]
Chase us : stories / Sean Ennis.
pages cm
ISBN 978-0-544-26300-0
I. Title.
PS3605.N56C43 2014
813'.6 — dc23
2013042346

Book design by Brian Moore

Printed in the United States of America
DOC 10 9 8 7 6 5 4 3 2 1

Stories in this collection have appeared in *Best New American Voices 2006*, the *Greensboro Review*, *Pinch*, the *Good Men Project*, *Tin House*, *Hot Metal Bridge*, *Construction*, *Down and Out*, the *Mississippi Review*, *Bayou*, *Talking Writing*, *Crazyhorse*, and *Fifty-Two Stories*.

For Mom and Dad

Contents

Going After Lovely

O N CHRISTMAS EVE, DAD came home from the mall and hammered up a bedsheet in the doorway to the living room. No one was allowed in, and there was crashing and cursing behind it. I had been scanning TV commercials on the small set in the kitchen for any last-minute gems I might have missed during my six weeks of Christmas requests. Mom was locking the windows, and my older sister, Lovely, was at the kitchen table, talking on the phone with her boyfriend, Roger, a kid who would mainly twist my ears whenever he saw me, saying, "Now hear this!"

When Mom saw the hanging sheet, she padded quickly back to the bathroom and ran the water in the tub. Lovely hung up the phone.

"You were listening, weren't you?" she said. "You're going to tell them."

I had no idea what she was talking about. I had just been watching the sheet, hoping for some clue about what was on the other side. Lovely headed toward the living room and pushed the sheet aside.

"Don't!" Dad yelled. "Get out!"

Lovely turned back, her face pinched with contempt. She turned the TV off as she walked out of the room and gave me the finger. I crept across the kitchen to turn it back on, but kept my eyes trained on the sheet.

Finally, Dad came out from behind the sheet and grabbed me by the arm. "I need your help," he said. "We have to put this together for Mom."

A dozen long sheets of frosted plastic, four fluorescent bulbs and rigs, and two big bags of potting soil were laid out on the carpet in the living room.

I recognized the equipment. It was an indoor greenhouse, something my mother had pointed out in the Sharper Image catalog, but I knew—even at twelve—that she didn't really want this. Dad had filled the small patch of dirt in our backyard with pachysandra specifically because they required no care.

The greenhouse was flimsy and everything snapped into place, but assembling it was still a two-man job. I held a piece, and Dad tried to slide another into it, cursing like I'd never heard him. The plastic wasn't cut perfectly, but he hammered the pieces together anyway. Then he hung the fluorescent bulbs, and I poured the soil into the bottom when he was finished. He plugged the lights in, and they buzzed and glowed a white-purple above the dirt. I guess the idea was that you could have a garden inside the house.

"She's gonna love this," Dad said.

I realize now that Mom was well on her way to becoming completely agoraphobic. She made only one daily, frantic trip outside, never at night. The rest of the time, she stayed deep inside the house, reaching into the dryer, organizing cans in a closet. She had stopped working in October. At the time, I thought it was a move made out of choice — that people either wanted to work or they didn't. But Mom was probably incapable of holding a job at that point.

Two other conspicuous packages sat in the living room: one for me and one for Lovely, I assumed. Dad always did his shopping on Christmas Eve, and as a result he bought everyone exactly what he thought they might want, no questions asked. It was a strange, vomiting kind of charity. He was helpless and well intentioned, working two jobs now, confused about why his family seemed to hate him.

But I didn't hate him. I think I just missed him.

Dad turned off all the lights in the living room except for the fluorescent bulbs hanging inside the greenhouse. He meant for it to be pretty, but it wasn't. It was like someone had put a pay phone in our living room. He looked disappointed for a second, as if he suddenly saw that the gift was ridiculous, and then he just switched off all the lights, and we went to bed.

Lovely came into my room and demanded to know what I'd helped Dad build. I wouldn't tell.

"Go in and look for yourself," I said, but I knew she wouldn't. Dad had scared her earlier. Scared me, too.

"It's something stupid for me, isn't it? A dollhouse or something. Know what I really want?" she said. "A backpack. A big sturdy backpack."

I didn't know why anyone would want that. She had been hinting all fall that she wanted a car, but even she knew that wasn't going to happen. At seventeen, her red hair and freckles were no longer cute, but she hadn't grown into her name yet either. It was part of why she was so angry, I think.

"Weird things are going on, little brother. I found Mom under her bed when I came home from school yesterday. She said she fell asleep. What do you think of that?"

I shrugged. I had seen Mom throw her car keys in the trash two days earlier. I took them out when she left the room and set them on the counter. I didn't mention that, though. I just said, "Don't sleep too late tomorrow. I want presents."

The next morning—Christmas—the sheet was still up in the living room, and we waited outside until Dad came down. Rather than pulling the sheet aside, he plucked at each nail until the curtain finally fell, and there, framed by the doorway and lit up by the sun through the windows, was the indoor greenhouse.

Mom approached it slowly, peering into it as if it might contain some sort of animal. It did look like a drained aquarium, eight feet high and four feet deep.

"What the heck's that?" Lovely said. "What's it do? Who's it for?"

"It's for Mom. It's a greenhouse," Dad said. "For inside."

Mom opened the see-through door and looked in and then looked back at Dad. He smiled nervously, teeth gritted, and made a "voilà!" gesture with his hands. She shut the door, and Dad handed her a small package. There were seeds inside, and Mom shuffled through the envelopes nonstop like they were playing cards.

I guess at that point Mom was on medication, too. She did seem fainter and fainter, almost blurry to look at, charged with a purpose none of us could understand and focused on something just above our heads and out of the frame.

Lovely opened her package from Dad; it was a telescope. She didn't hide her displeasure. Dad gave me an archery set. Since we lived in a row home in Northeast Philadelphia, there was no sensible place to shoot an arrow. Also, there were no stars above the lights of the city, telescope or not. A brown smog hung above the neighborhood that brightened occasionally under a full moon. Our stars were only as high as the street lamps, the floodlights at car dealerships, the blinkers at the tops of factory smokestacks.

And when Lovely and I looked around, we realized there were no other presents to open. Christmas was over.

Lovely ran out and slammed the door to her room, leaving the telescope box behind, unopened. Dad walked Mom over to the couch and whispered to her about what seeds would be best to plant first. I went to my room, got changed, and took the bow and arrows outside to see what I could do.

All the other kids in the neighborhood were riding their new bikes and playing with their new remote-control cars in the street. I had never shot an arrow in my life—had never even thought of the possibility—and I was excited. Targets hung everywhere: street signs, parked cars, the occasional city tree. A thin groove at the bottom of each arrow seemed to fit the string, so I settled one in and pulled it back, but the tension became too much and I let go with both hands. The contraption fell to the ground with a clang, and all the neighborhood kids looked up. I had *something,* for sure.

After a few more tries, I managed to launch an arrow across the street without much speed. It hit the Kramers' garage door with a thud. Everyone cheered. My friend Clip dropped his new hockey stick and followed me around, begging for a turn.

When I went back inside, Mom was on her knees with a little spade, planting seeds in the living room. Lovely's door was still closed, but Dad had taken the telescope out of the box and was setting it up. He pointed to my bow.

"How's it work?" he said. "Kill any Indians?"

Mom looked up. "The Indians used arrows. Cowboys used guns." She'd taught grade school before she quit.

"Right, right," Dad said. "Well, maybe there's fighting between Indians. They did that, too."

Mom wasn't listening. "But no matter what," she said, "all those things still fall out of the sky. Right on your head. A person shouldn't get involved." Then she climbed farther into the greenhouse. She said a lot of things in those days that we ignored.

I said, "I hit the Kramers' garage from over here."

"Good. They need to be brought down a few notches." Dad turned the end of the telescope toward me. "Here, look at this. Wanna see Pluto?"

I looked in and saw that Dad had cut out a space scene from the telescope box, taped it to the far window, and lined the scope up perfectly. A flying saucer was frozen in front of a green planet with rings, and moons and stars were everywhere in the background.

"Just kidding," he said and tore the picture off the window. Lovely hadn't even seen what he had planned for her, and I could tell he was sad about it. He slapped the end of the telescope, and it spun and wobbled on its hinge. "Well, merry Christmas, family."

Mom hadn't bought us any presents. This was clear, though Dad made no mention of it—maybe because he was surprised, too. In the past, we just shrugged at his bizarre holiday attempts: the rock tumbler Dad got me the year before was unopened in the garage, and Lovely had never plugged in the massaging chair he gave her. But we were always happy because Mom got us all the right things. And if we were happy, Dad was happy. Not this year.

Lovely, insulted and incredulous, told me privately that Dad could use the telescope to look up his own ass. She said she was going to run away from "this fucking crazy house." And though Lovely was only five years older than me, she seemed infinitely wiser and, better yet, meaner—mean enough to survive, to cut all of us out of her life, just like that. I still felt too tied and dependent to follow her, though I was beginning to understand that I was only one or two people away from being completely on my own.

But unlike Lovely and her telescope, I liked my archery set and was getting better at using it. The back of the package was a target, so I tied it to the telephone pole outside our house. That week after Christmas, I spent most of my time outside with the set, and scored two bull's-eyes. I didn't shoot the arrows at other kids, like Clip had encouraged me to. Instead, I stayed focused on the target and shot hidden from behind different obstacles on the street—parked cars, trash cans, the occasional city tree. I liked the target because it cataloged each good shot with a ragged but unmistakable hole. I was the Indian Dad said I was, always aiming, on the attack, and never at home.

Lovely went to a party on New Year's Eve and never came back. Dad was devastated, mainly because of a cruel note she had written that he never showed me. She had taped it to the far window across from the telescope, and the next night, after a day of worrying, Dad saw what it said, real big.

Mom rarely came out of her indoor greenhouse. She invented tasks that needed to be performed inside it since nothing actually needed to be done. It would still be weeks before anything appeared above ground, if at all, so she Windexed the walls and tightened the lightbulbs. I was beginning to worry that she slept in the greenhouse, but I never stayed up late enough to check. Plus, Dad was staying in the living room late, too, using the telescope at night to scour the neighborhood for Lovely.

. . .

My block was just different shades of gray: the row homes were whitish-gray, the asphalt dark gray, cars brownish-gray with soot. But my arrows had color, red tips backed with orange and yellow and green feathers. Shooting them was like planting flowers.

Some of the other fathers in the neighborhood came to talk to my dad about me. The street was littered with arrows at this point, some stuck too high in a telephone pole or tree for me to get down. The fathers were worried about the safety of their kids and pets and property.

They were also upset because all their kids wanted archery sets.

Dad ignored their complaints. Every Friday, there was a new box of arrows on my bed, and a new present for Lovely in her room as well—left unopened, of course. When the fathers came to the door, Dad rarely took his eye from the telescope, but instead just aimed the telescope in the direction of the visitor and never spoke. Then he would turn the eyepiece toward Mom for a second—always buried in the greenhouse—then point it back out the window in search of some clue. After this happened a few times, the other fathers stopped coming.

"They've got nothing better to do than worry about our problems?" Dad would say. "Must be nice."

School started back up, and Lovely still wasn't home. Outside, winter came on harder, but miraculously, tiny green buds began pushing their way through the soil in the greenhouse. Mom was delighted and talked only about this event. Conversations at dinner—now prepared by Dad—were strictly about the new plant food she was going to try and the centimeters of progress each plant made. She took her meals seated in the doorway to her greenhouse.

Pushed out of the living room by the greenhouse and telescope activity, I spent most evenings in my bedroom. Some of the fathers on the block had warned me that they would take the bow and arrows if they saw me with them, even if my own dad wouldn't. I hadn't done any real damage or hurt anyone, but I was plotting now.

The first time I shot an arrow into my bedroom door, it made so much noise I thought for sure Mom and Dad would hear, but no one came. After that, I drew a bull's-eye on every wall.

"Where's Lovely?" Mom said.

She talked to me a little. Her voice was muffled through the plastic walls of the greenhouse. "You know, don't you?"

"She went to that party," I said. I was walking through the living room, dropping off my schoolbooks. I tried to avoid that room as much as I could.

"Two weeks ago. She told you she was going to leave, didn't she?"

I shrugged. "She said this is a 'fucking crazy house.'"

Mom pressed against the plastic. "Do *you* think so?"

Dad was in the kitchen, fixing dinner, humming his cooking song. I knew he wouldn't like this conversation.

"I think it's not that bad." I started gathering my bow and arrows, making to leave and end the conversation.

"You like your present, though, don't you? I told Dad you would. I know you're an angry boy."

I had never thought that at the time. But I suppose I was.

"When Lovely comes back, we can all live in here," Mom said. She was squatting in the dirt with her shoes off. "Dad could put a lock on the door, and you could protect us with the arrows, and Lovely would watch everybody with the telescope and tell us what's happening out there. I'll grow the food."

I wanted to ask her if she had actually picked out the presents for us that Christmas, but Dad came through the door, carrying cauliflower soup and crackers, and Mom turned off the lights in the greenhouse. She took the bowl and receded into the dark.

"Your mom is busy, Sitting Bull," Dad said. "Let her eat her supper."

I hustled out of the room, knowing Mom's plan for the future was crazy, though it might come true.

That night — a school night — Dad knocked on my door. I was actually aiming at the bull's-eye on the door when he came, so it's a good thing. By then my white walls were practically black with holes. I fantasized about the day I would lean on one of the battered walls and it would fall over.

"Know what I think about all this?" Dad said.

"My arrows?"

"No. Lovely. I think she's with that Roger." The suction from the telescope's eyepiece had left a sweaty pucker around his right eye. "I found his house with the scope. I say we go get her. Right now." He pointed to the bow. "Bring that."

I bundled up quickly, thrilled to be a part of Dad's plan. I collected as many arrows as I could carry and found Dad in the living room, in the doorway of the greenhouse, whispering to Mom. He kissed her cheek, and then we headed out into the cold.

We walked a block or two without speaking. I noticed he was looking around the neighborhood at all the arrows I had planted.

"Getting pretty good with that thing, I see," Dad said.

I shrugged.

"You miss your sister?"

"Not all the time."

"I'm gonna fix this family," he said. "If I have to do it one person at a damn time, then so be it. You hear me?" He was smiling when he said this.

"Do you want me to shoot Roger?" I asked. It wasn't an impossible thing for me to imagine doing. Once, to impress Lovely, Roger had choked me until I passed out.

"I want you to come as close to shooting him as you can without doing it. Understand? I won't be made a fool of by someone that rides a damn skateboard."

It suddenly occurred to me that Dad hadn't gotten any presents at all that Christmas because Mom usually bought our gifts for him, too.

"I'm sorry I didn't get you a Christmas gift, Dad. Mom usually—"

"I know. It's okay. Consider this it."

We got to Roger's house at about nine that night. It looked exactly like our own except the trim around the garage was white instead of black. Dad banged on the door, and Roger's dad opened it. He was dressed in a white undershirt with yellowed armpits, and dress pants—an out-of-shape man, but still bigger than Dad. I recognized him as one of the men who wanted to take my bow and arrows from me.

"We came for Lovely," Dad said. I held the bow slack at my side, but with an arrow notched, ready to go.

"What's Lovely?"

"My daughter. I think she's here."

Roger's dad just shrugged. It didn't seem like he was lying.

"Can I at least speak with Roger?"

"Roger's asleep. He has school tomorrow. What's this about?" He looked down at me. "This is your kid with the bow and arrow?"

I glared at Roger's dad from behind my own. I was waiting for some signal from Dad to shoot this guy in the belly. We hadn't decided on one, but I assumed I would know it when it came.

"This is important," Dad said. "My daughter has been missing for two weeks."

"Hey, call the cops. And keep that bow and arrow away from around here or I'll snap it in two pieces." As he slammed the door, I heard Roger's dad mutter, "Fucking nuts, all of them."

I realized then that my family was gaining a reputation in the neighborhood. I looked at Dad and saw the same thought flash across his face. Of course, he had called the police. What was he, crazy?

"Come on," he said.

He led me by the shoulder across the street, and then we stopped and turned around. He pointed to a lighted window on the second floor of Roger's house. "See up there? That's where that nice man sleeps. Think you can hit it with one of those?"

I considered the trajectory and factored in my puny sense of wind effects. I nodded.

"Well, smash that damn cowboy's window, Geronimo!"

I pulled back and launched. The arrow hung in the air until the tip tapped the window with a *plink!* and fell into the shrubs. Dad cheered and picked me up and spun me around. "That's the way to do it!" he sang. "Score one for us, finally!"

As we walked toward home, I heard the window open behind us and Roger's dad yelled, "Okay! I'll call the cops *for* you, asshole! Have fun in jail!"

It didn't matter. Dad kept recounting the shot like it had been a field goal kicked in the last seconds of the game. He made an arrow out of his hand and, whistling, sailed it into his other hand like it was the window. "Boom!" he yelled when the two touched.

· · ·

But Dad stopped cheering when he saw the police car in front of our house.

"What the hell?" he said. "How'd they get here so quick?"

I thought I should hide the bow, but was afraid to part with it. I considered another Wild West fight — their bullets and my arrows. I readied an arrow and looked up at Dad.

"Easy, Tonto. Let's see what this is about before you make them start pushing up daisies."

I hung back while Dad talked with the cops. I wondered if I would be going to jail. A young police officer came over to talk with me.

"That's some toy you got there, buddy," he said. "Are you a good shot?"

I shrugged, not wanting to implicate myself.

"I bet that was a Christmas present. What else did you get for Christmas, little man?"

"Nothing," I told him.

"Well, don't worry. Everything's gonna be all right. Why don't we hang around out here for a while, and you show me how that thing works?"

Dad disappeared into our house. I walked up and down the block, pulling arrows out of everything I could reach while the cop tried to make conversation.

Finally, Dad came out and called, "Hey, Last of the Mohicans! Come over here." He gave me a big hug and thanked the cops. I overheard our neighbor telling one of them, "I didn't know what else to do. All that screaming . . ." The frame to our front door was splintered, and the lock lay on the ground. Dad took me aside.

"Listen, your mom got a little upset that we were gone for so long tonight. She thought we left like your sister. I guess she misunderstood me." He had a phony-looking smile on his face that was ready to crack at any minute.

"But she's in the tub now, so I need you to be quiet and go on to bed."

I nodded and went inside, the drama of the evening slowly deflating. Dirt from the greenhouse was spread throughout the living room; one of the lightbulbs was smashed. I headed for my room, hoping Dad would be in to check on Mom soon.

He walked past my door on the way to the bathroom and peeked in.

"Good job tonight, Sitting Bull. See you in the morning."

I lay in bed, listening to the tub splashing a little next door, and the calm, indecipherable words Dad spoke to Mom. I decided I would sleep on the floor that night, naked as an Indian, and imagine that I lay in the dirt and there was no ceiling above me either, but instead that picture Dad had cut out on Christmas—all those stars and moons and planets.

Over the next few days, Mom had visitors. All the mothers from the neighborhood came and admired her indoor greenhouse—hastily reassembled by Dad—and made small talk. Mom was pleased. Dad strutted among all these women, his phony smile seeming a little more genuine now, serving drinks and snacks. He demonstrated the telescope for the other mothers, even played the same gag with the window he'd tried with Lovely. Mom's pallor was moving back into a pinkish sort of gray, and Dad winked at me over her shoulder whenever she said something that sounded normal. She still held most of her conversations half inside the greenhouse, but her plants were coming up now and seemed like they might actually need her attention.

One night, half awake, I swore I heard them both go back to their bedroom to sleep, giggling a little, and at a decent hour.

• • •

These moments of peace couldn't last, though. Lovely was still missing, close to three weeks by then. The police came by every once in a while, but Dad just put his head in his hands after they left. He still felt, in his own strange way, that this was his case to solve. With Mom doing better, in a sense, and busy in the greenhouse, Dad started taking his telescope to different spots in the neighborhood to look for my sister. I followed along and would shoot arrows for distance wherever he pointed the scope, hoping just to tap Lovely on her butt, reminding her to come home.

The police arrived one night when we were perched on top of Arnold Street, the tallest hill in the development. The cops recognized us and were kind, aware of all our dilemmas. The same young cop winked at me over his partner's shoulder. Dad, though, got angry.

"If you deputies would do your job, I wouldn't have to be out here looking for my daughter in the freezing cold!"

They hinted that Dad could be arrested for a couple of things and should at least call off the search for the evening. Dad relented, muttering under his breath—a frightening new habit of his. They insisted on driving us back home in the squad car, a move that my dad declared "ridiculous pageantry." But it was obvious that the police's patience with our family was wearing thin. The telescope barely fit in the back seat.

I started playing a new game with the bow and arrows. I would shoot straight up in the air and stand perfectly still, waiting for the arrow to fall, a game of chance. I didn't get hit, but came very close a few times. If the arrow fell down the right way, its weighted tip would bury itself deep in the ground.

After a long school night of searching for Lovely, Dad began looking down the wrong end of the telescope in the living room and got newly amazed.

"Take a look at this!" he said. "Try this end!"

Looking down the opposite end made everything smaller—the entirety of our living room appeared to sit at the end of a long, dark corridor. Dad was in there, an inch high now, manically waving, like he had actually been shrunk.

As I turned the scope, Dad maneuvered to stay within the boundaries of the lens, as if to keep his small stature. He smiled weakly like I was taking his picture.

"Look at your mother, too," he said.

I panned to the greenhouse and there she was: a woman inside a house inside a room inside a telescope. A strange sight. I imagined shooting a tiny arrow down that long corridor to plink against that tiny greenhouse.

"See what I mean?" Dad said.

I nodded. "Look at me," I said. I posed and drew an arrow back in the bow. I tried to look fierce as Dad looked through the telescope.

"That's perfect." He held me in it for a moment and then swung the telescope toward Mom. "Now you!"

She smiled between her plants, cupped a daisy in her hands, and batted her eyelashes. We all laughed. The snow picked up outside and scraped the windows, but it was warm inside and I felt safe in that house for the first time in a while.

If only it had been that easy. If something could have shrunk our trouble into something small and containable, something funny, we would have been okay. But that was the wrong way to see things. And when the phone rang in the kitchen, it was like an alarm clock—crisp and abrasive—waking us up out of our dreams.

· · ·

The call wasn't good, like most that come so late at night. Lovely from a train station in Baltimore, needing money. Or a faraway aunt to say Lovely had shown up in the middle of the night with a strange friend, only to disappear in the morning. Or the police. I forget which call came first, there got to be so many.

I lost interest in the bow and arrows by that March, never hitting anything worth much. I tried other forms of violence over the years: cracked skateboards, junior high fistfights, gallons of gin. The arrows were just a good start.

The greenhouse stayed up another year and became filled with more and more monstrous plants—sunflowers, strange corn, even what I think was marijuana. But when Mom fashioned a lock for its door, Dad finally intervened.

That night he knocked on my door and I came out to the living room, groggy with sleep. Mom stood in the greenhouse, threatening with her spade, the door padlocked from the inside.

"Your sister called again," he said and then gestured toward the lock. I saw the problem. "Don't think I haven't thought of leaving myself. We could, you know, you and I."

He rooted through his toolbox, which was lying open on the floor. "I've been trying. You know that. But then I think maybe I should just let them all go ahead and get what they want. Some things can't be fixed, I'm sure you've realized. Can't shoot it. Can't even be nice to it." He pulled a hammer from the box. "I mean, when I tear this thing down, your mom may come at me with that spade."

"She won't," I said, but I wasn't sure. Mom's hair was matted with mud, her hands cut and bleeding. "And Lovely will come back, too, Dad."

"She might. But I got news for you. We're all nuts. You

shouldn't be the last to know that. When I take this thing apart, you should get out of here. That's why I got you up."

I knew Lovely probably wouldn't come back. And now the greenhouse, that last monument to good intentions gone awful, had to come down, too.

Dad approached with the hammer, and Mom slammed the blade of her spade into the plastic on level with his face. Dad looked back at me, sunk the claw between the greenhouse's wall and roof, and said, "Run."

This Is Suicide

S UICIDE IS A GAME you play against a wall with a tennis ball. Some kids call it Homicide or Slaughterball, but that's wrong. You need at least three people to start, and when it's your turn, you have to catch the ball and throw it back at the wall. If you drop it, you have to run to the wall and say "Suicide!" before someone else picks up the ball and hits you with it. If you're hit, you're out and have to sit off in the grass at the edge of the lot.

The Arboretum has the best wall we know of, the side of the Visitors' Center building. No one ever visits, and the parking lot's always empty. The Wall is cinder block and painted dark green to go with the special trees. You can use the bathroom and water fountain inside the Visitors' Center if you ever have to.

We're eleven. We've had beer and cigarettes, but don't like them. We don't drive either. Or chase girls or read or go to that stupid summer camp.

· · ·

We started a gang. It's summertime, and we are the Rattle-snakes. Our color is green like the Wall and like the special trees at the Arboretum. When we see one another, we make the sign. Right elbow in the left palm and bend your wrist into a snake. Make it hiss.

There's five of us now. Me, Clip, Warren, Milk, Eric. That's enough because there's no other gang to fight yet. But Warren, our Magician, predicts they will come in orange, so we watch for that.

Back when Roger was a Rattlesnake, Clip called him the Prince. I was Lookout. Milk and Eric were fatter and both called Muscles. Warren stole the tennis balls from his Dad and was called Treasurer, but he hated it. Clip was Fangs. We graf-fitied the Wall with our gang names. There are old scratches in the Wall from before, and we pretended they were our dads' old gang names.

We don't go to the summer camp at the Arboretum even though our moms paid for it—crap like nature walks, and picking up trash to recycle. One of the counselors always comes around the Wall to see if we want to look for dino-saur bones or learn judo with the rest of the campers. We call him Chief Big Homo. Clip doesn't ever stop playing when the Chief comes and throws pretty close to his head. And if Clip throws, then Warren has to catch it or he has to run. Then if Warren throws, I have to catch. The game keeps going. It can't stop as long as someone's throwing.

The Chief tries to talk while we play, but no one listens. He tries to talk to Milk and Eric, who are out and sitting in the grass at the edge of the lot. They watch the game through the Chief's legs. Eventually, we all start hissing at him, and he leaves, saying stupid things like, "Have it your way, dudes, you're missing the boat. We're feeding our pet Venus flytrap today." I think his real name is Edward.

Chief Big Homo wears a fishing vest with lures and medals stuck all over it, but there's no water in the Arboretum. He wears tan shorts with lots of pockets and hairy legs sticking out. He goes to college and doesn't know that we go to the Arboretum at night when we're not supposed to. We told him we're a gang, and he laughed. I wouldn't mind so much seeing that Venus flytrap eat a piece of hamburger meat, but Clip won't allow it.

The blacktop is hot and sticks to our shoes. The broken glass on it looks like the stars in space. Dad woke me up one night earlier in the summer to show me a meteor shower and told me, "Next time this happens, I'll be dead." But he was facing the wrong way and every meteor fell behind him. He had set up a camera and just got pictures of the black night. We've all seen our fathers embarrassed like this, but still, we do have each other.

And we make mistakes like our fathers, too. Clip hit Warren in the back of the head with the ball, and Warren threw up. There was a big lump. It was from the game and you're not supposed to throw at somebody's head, but we pretended it was from a gang fight—even Warren did. He had to lie down on the grass at the edge of the lot. Then Warren got weird and called from the grass that he wanted his new gang name to be Electro. Clip said, "No way, Treasurer," but this was when Warren started seeing the future and Clip started calling him Magician.

The first time Warren saw the future, he warned us that the Rattlesnakes would be betrayed. We looked at everybody, but Warren couldn't say who. It was Roger, we found out later and should've known. Warren says there's a buzz and his ears pop and then the future is like watching a TV with a sheet over his head. I didn't believe him then, but now I do.

. . .

The Chief brings five kids from the camp to our Wall in the afternoon, saying, "How about this? If we beat you at handball, you'll come to the camp for a day?" We're all staring at the one camper who has a purple birthmark on his face. Clip calls this one Raisin.

"No one is playing handball, Chief. This is Suicide," Clip tells him. "There're no teams either."

Clip holds the ball now. The game has stopped. Milk and Eric get up off the grass at the edge of the lot. They're always the first ones out. They are brothers. Clip says it is genetic.

Then we all see it at the same time. One of the campers the Chief brought wears an orange jersey. It's Roger. We all look at Warren and start to sweat — the other gang has shown up. Clip hits Roger in the mouth with the ball, and the blood won't stop spurting. We all scatter. Raisin throws our ball on the roof of the Visitors' Center. The Chief is almost crying on top of Roger, and finally he picks him up and brings him into the Center. I didn't think Clip would do that.

At home, Dad hides in the bathroom until his food is on the plate and then takes it back to the bathroom. I wash my hands three times in hot water or else I'm not allowed to eat. I have to count out loud to thirty each time, while Mom talks to my sister, Lovely, about *Wheel of Fortune.* I cough and Mom accuses me of smoking cigarettes. Dad puts his plate in the dishwasher and heads back down the hallway to the garage and sits in the back seat of the car until everyone is asleep. He reads a magazine called *Beckett Baseball Card Price Guide,* though Mom threw out all his baseball cards a long time ago. I go to the garage and get in the driver's seat of the car and tell Dad about the new gang at the Arboretum. He's working on his cards. He's drawing copies of the ones Mom trashed on old cardboard boxes with India ink. He remembers the photos and stats by heart.

"Boys fighting boys is like pouring water from one glass into another," Dad tells me. "You'll find there are worse things worth worrying about."

He takes his X-Acto knife and starts cutting the cardboard.

"This is Pete Rose's rookie card, my son and copy," he says. "A woman ruined him, and he resorted to fixing the game he loved in disgust. It's worth six thousand dollars."

If you throw the ball and the next person catches it in the air, you have to run, too. Back in June when our moms found out about the Rattlesnakes, they sent our dads down to get us at the Arboretum, but the dads just watched us play. The Chief had called and told our moms that we weren't going to the camp that cost four hundred and fifty dollars. Milk and Eric were out in the grass at the edge of the lot when our dads showed up, so we let them back in the game. We started over.

It was after dinner, and the sun was looking right at the moon like a showdown. My dad brought his magazine with him. Clip's wore a neck brace. Warren's carried a bottle of sunscreen, and Milk and Eric's wore rubber gloves and a surgical mask because he's afraid of contamination. They didn't say anything, but we knew why they were there.

Roger was still with us then, and the Rattlesnakes were six. He didn't have a dad, but Roger always won. He threw the hardest and was impossible to hit with the ball. He beat us all that night, but with mean shots to the head and privates to embarrass us. Each dad cried a little when his son got out, but there was no talking. They would not step onto the lot. Roger finally hit Clip in the ear, and the game was over. Our heads and dicks and butts hurt from it all.

The dads left. The moon pushed the sun down, and the lights came on. We stayed.

That was the night Clip ran Roger out of the gang because

he whipped us all so bad in front of our dads. He chased him
through the Arboretum but could never catch him. It was a
great race. Across the paths. Over the special bushes. They
knocked over a birdbath, and we followed as close as we could.
Then Clip ran into the camp's volleyball net and Roger disappeared into the special trees. There was heat lightning but no
rain. Orange flashes in a black night.

Our dads approved when we whispered and told them
about what Clip did. They didn't like Roger's dad either, we all
learned, whoever he was.

There's a good moon up tonight at the Arboretum. A green
moon, we call it, but really it's orange with humidity and pollution. We don't talk about that. Good things come green. Clip
scratches the name "The Prince" off our wall. We play Suicide
and try to talk, but it's a fast game. Wherever you catch the
ball is where you have to throw it from. It can't bounce before
it hits the Wall or else you have to run. If you want to talk, it's
best to have the ball or else you might miss your turn.

Warren makes more predictions. He tells me that I will have
a son, the greatest Rattlesnake of all. Part kid, part snake even.
It makes me feel a little better.

Then there's hooting in the trees, and they run through
our game, at least eight of them. Raisin knocks Milk and Eric
over from behind. Roger snatches our ball and roofs it on the
Visitors' Center. They are a gang. We hear them say, "Go Mongooses!" Then they disappear down the driveway and back
into our dark neighborhood.

That was our only ball and things don't look good. Milk's
elbow is cut up, and he suggests we just play freeze tag instead
because we can play that anywhere, like in front of one of our
houses. Clip tells him to shut up. He says, let him think.

Without a ball, we all just walk home, but in pairs so we

don't get jumped. Except Clip, who goes by himself and cuts through the back of the Arboretum instead of walking on the sidewalks under the street lamps.

My sister, Lovely, got her woman's period, and Mom makes a cake with sour cream in it. Dad pulls the car out of the garage and sits in it down at the curb. I eat the cake and hear about maxi pads with wings. I don't care about anything but the Rattlesnakes. I work on the design for the jackets we're going to make for the winter.

Lovely comes in my room and asks if I've ever rubbed on a girl's chest. I throw a tennis ball at her, and she says it hurt her new uterus. When I am old and thirty, I will be a Rattlesnake. There will be a thousand of us. And my son, the best Rattlesnake ever, better than Clip even. Lovely starts wearing makeup. I call her Ugly instead.

Tennis balls go flat and lose their bounce if they get wet or stepped on too much. New ones are sealed in a vacuum and pop off the wall. They thwack. Warren has bad nightmares and a concussion. His mom calls my mom. Clip cuts himself on purpose. Milk and Eric sleep on their knees and elbows now. Their mom calls my mom. I'm in a bad mood, too. The moms are talking in a language I can't understand.

We don't play freeze tag, we still play Suicide, and we don't see the Mongooses for a couple days. Warren still tries to play, but he says his eyes are funny and can never catch. Now he just waits for the ball to stop rolling and then picks it up and throws from wherever it lands. It's not the same.

Lovely wears a bra now, and they are all over the house. Dad has started smoking cigarettes and uses his magazine to move the bras if they are in his way. Everyone talks about Lovely's boobs, how great. Dad filled one of the cups with cigarette ash; then Mom made him do all the laundry, even the nice tablecloths and my bedsheets.

I'm still waiting for my man's period. Nothing ever comes. I lie on my stomach, but there's only a bright wash of shock that goes through me and then I have to sleep. Everything stays dry. I think of girls like Lovely to make it happen, but not her exactly. I don't know any girls, but I know I need to make this work.

A woman with a yellow notepad comes and talks to us at the Wall. Dr. Hesterwill. Her hair is short and she wears a suit like a man's with a skirt. She asks why we're not at camp with the rest of the kids.

"We have our gang," Clip tells her. "Chief Big Homo wants to grab our butts, but we won't let him."

She writes it down. "What does the gang do?"

"Plays Suicide and fights the Mongooses." Clip thinks she's a reporter from the TV. She keeps writing and then starts underlining. She looks worried and goes around the Wall back to the camp. Clip pumps his hips at her while her back is turned. If you cheat at Suicide, you get an a-ball. You have to put your hands on the wall and stick your butt out, and whoever you cheated gets a free shot. We all know the best thing to do is to bounce it on the way up and catch him in the nuts.

The woman with the notepad is from the Chief's college, Warren says, because he sees something about her in the future. I spot her car in the lot. Milk and Eric circle around to protect us.

"The Rattlesnakes don't go to college," Clip says. We all make the sign and hiss. Mom paid four hundred and fifty dollars for me to go to that camp, but I won't do that either. The ball hits the woman's car a lot while we play and makes little craters in the hood. If it ever rains, the water will puddle and rust it right through.

We know Chief Big Homo teaches a judo class at the camp, and we're worried about the Mongooses. We don't know how to fight because none of us have ever been in one. The Mongooses have drawn a snake in a dress on our wall.

When I asked Dad to teach me how to fight, he took me into the bathroom and brought a chair from the kitchen. He shut the door behind us and jammed the chair under the knob so no one could open it.

"There you go," he said. "If I said that I wanted to show you this, I would be lying. But you asked." He let me look for a minute at what he had rigged up.

"But in the parking lot?" I asked. "There's no doors and no chairs."

"Oh. There. Well, here's my face. Smash it if that's what you want to do." He knelt down and pointed right to his nose. We stared at each other for a long while. Then he got up and moved the chair. Then he went to the garage.

Mom said, "What were you two doing?"

We're out on the lot, and Clip calls the Rattlesnakes "desperate." The sun hates us with heat. The Mongooses own the trees. Clip takes a safety pin and cuts a little snake into his arm. He fills the cut with ink from a cracked ballpoint pen. It's raw and black and red and doesn't look like a snake at all anymore. "Now you," he says and gives the pin to Warren, who looks at all of us and then starts to cut. He pours the ink in but has an allergic reaction. His face blows up, and he has to go home. He didn't see that in the future.

Warren's mom calls my mom that night. Then my mom strips off all my clothes, looking for a tattoo. Dad is honking the horn out in the car the whole time. Her hands are cold, and everything down there tries to crawl back up inside me. But later that night, when I am lying on my stomach, trying to make it work, I think a little of standing naked in front of Mom.

We haven't fought the Mongooses yet. They only run through our game and knock us over and steal our ball. But they make kicks and yelp when they do, showing off their judo. Roger has an orange bandana tied around his head and no shirt. He's a small kid with sharp teeth, but I think that Clip is scared of him. I know I am. He gets in Clip's face when they run through and says, "Motherfucker, motherfucker!"

Milk and Eric suggest making a trip wire across the parking lot, but where do we get wire? Clip thinks he can get a knife. Warren says, "Poison. Poison gas."

Roger dates Lovely now, and Clip calls it "political." Roger comes to my house, and they go for walks before it gets too dark. Lovely's boobs are sticking out and up. Dad yells "No!" from inside the car, but no one can hear him. The windows are rolled up and locked. The car is a light-blue one that Mom picked out, and he's not even allowed to move the seat. His mouth is fixed in a silent no.

Later, Lovely comes into my room wearing an orange handkerchief around her neck to hide her hickeys. She says, "Roger knows judo and taught me this," and grabs my arm and ties it in a knot behind my back. I don't want to, but I start to cry. She leaves, laughing.

I tell the Rattlesnakes about the judo Roger taught my sister. I show the bruises. If you miss the Wall when you throw, you have to run and someone else chases the ball. You can't do it on purpose or it's an a-ball. If the ball goes too far behind the

Wall, you have to relay the ball to someone else. You have to call relay, and someone has to accept it. That's the only time that Suicide is maybe like a team game.

When I get home that night, Dr. Hesterwill is at the table with my mom, drinking tea. I can hear Dad whimpering in the bathroom like a puppy.

"Tell us exactly what's going on at the Arboretum," Dr. Hesterwill says.

I don't really know. So I tell them what I do know.

"I carry the seed for the greatest Rattlesnake to come."

"Edward told you this?"

"No, the Magician told me."

"That's what you call Edward?"

"No, we call him Chief Big Homo."

Mom yelps. Dr. Hesterwill takes out a doll and asks me to point to where he touched me. I say he hasn't. Mom takes all my clothes off and finds the bruises Lovely gave me. Dad keeps flushing the toilet in the bathroom to cover up his sobs. Lovely walks in and laughs. Naked again in front of Mom and Dr. Hesterwill, I think about how I will make a son since I think it would go something like this.

Clip and Roger finally fight. Roger brings the Mongooses to the Wall and says, "Let's go, you and me, Clip, no one else, motherfucker." We're scared. Clip walks straight for Roger and pulls out a small knife we didn't know he had. Roger knocks it from his hand and ties Clip's arms in a knot behind his back, the same way Lovely did to me. He knees Clip in the back until he falls, and then gets on top of him with his knees on his chest. The air is out of Clip now, and Raisin picks up the knife and gives it to Roger. We Rattlesnakes don't do anything.

"You were gonna stab me, motherfucker? I'll stab you!"

Then the Chief comes running and screaming onto the lot. Roger drops the knife, and the Mongooses run down the driveway out into the neighborhood. Clip gets up and is never the same. The Chief takes him into the Visitors' Center.

Dad brings me into the bathroom and locks the door behind me. He has his cards out. "This is Don Mattingly. He was the best hitter in the game but never won a World Series. Do you understand?"

I don't and tell him instead that my son will be the greatest Rattlesnake ever.

"That may be true," Dad says, "but how do you plan on making him? With whom?"

I give it some thought but come up blank.

"I made you a card, too," he says. "Here."

On the front of my card there's a drawing of me on the pitcher's mound, the ball in my glove and a snake on my hat. I'm checking the runner at first base over my shoulder. The runner looks like Mom, and the first basemen looks like Dad. His glove is open and stretched toward me, trying to keep Mom from stealing. The back has my birthday, height, weight, and all my grades from school, term by term.

The Chief is so sad. I go into the Visitors' Center to use the bathroom, and he's mixing vodka into his Gatorade at the sink. A dirty blue jay feather is pinned to his baseball hat.

"You kids," he says, and there is a bubble in his throat that pops. "Won't you just come to camp? I'm going to be kicked out of school. Roger and his friends have stolen all the archery sets and hidden them in the trees. They don't listen to me." He slouches down between the sinks.

"Will you teach us to fight if we come to the camp?"

"This was just supposed to be a stupid summer internship."

"Will you teach us to fight?"

"Your damn mothers?" he says.

"Everyone," I say.

Mom and Dad are fighting. Dad has the chair propped up against the door to the bathroom, and I have to go real bad. Lovely follows me out into the yard, and I can't make it happen. Inside, Mom has gotten down on her knees and is shouting at Dad through the crack between the bottom of the bathroom door and the floor. They're fighting about us kids.

Roger shows up on our porch, bouncing one of our tennis balls. The Mongooses already had their jackets made, and I haven't even finished our design yet. The back of his jacket has an orange mongoose chomping on a snake. He has the collar turned up, but it's July and too hot for that. I tell him so through the screen door.

"Anytime, anyplace, Rattlesnake," he says. He throws the ball at the screen, and I flinch.

Lovely bursts from behind me out the door and leaves even though it's too late for her to go out. Mom has set up a chair now, too, outside the bathroom door, and is reading from a notebook full of problems she has with my dad.

It's late into August now and school's coming. I can see it like a storm on the radar. The fight is over for the night, and Dad goes out to the garage. Mom snores in her complaining chair. I go out my window because the Rattlesnakes are in trouble and in need. The moon is up and orange and pulsing under the clouds.

Bats are chirping in the special trees, and they sound like bells. It has never rained once this summer, and the ground is cracked, and the grass is like hay. The Visitors' Center is locked and dark, but the lights in the parking lot are on and filled with bugs. I stack the trash cans and climb on its roof to have a look.

Tennis balls like lights are spread across the roof in bright green points. I'm out in space, floating with the stars, and I collect them. The ones Raisin and Roger have roofed. The ones we threw ourselves by mistake. There must be a hundred.

I can see a lot from the roof. Lovely is walking with Roger on the sidewalk, his hand down the back of her pants. I see the Chief in his car, working on his thesis, his computer plugged into the cigarette lighter. I can see through windows in the neighborhood and in them our dads are begging and our moms are on the phone. Something bad is coming. The air is like the hot breath of a dog.

The next morning at the Arboretum, I show the Rattlesnakes the trash can I filled up with our lost tennis balls and they're proud of me. Warren dips his hand in the trash can and says there are a hundred and eight balls. We play for a while, and Clip is the first one out. He sits on the grass at the edge of the lot, looking into the trees.

The Chief comes to the Wall in his car. The back seat is filled with boxes of books and clothes. I think he lives in there now. He says if we teach him to play Suicide, he'll teach us to fight. The Mongooses don't listen to him anymore. He still carries his school bag even though he has been kicked out of school. Inside the bag, he shows us five new cans of tennis balls and gives one to each of us.

We all look at Clip for an answer, but he just shrugs. Since the fight, he has changed. He says, "I don't care." Warren and Milk and Eric all look at me. I think of Warren's prediction, my son.

"Okay," I say. "Suicide is a game you play against a wall with a tennis ball. Some kids call it Homicide or Slaughterball, but that's wrong. You need at least three people to start, and when it is your turn, you have to catch the ball and throw it back at the wall. If you drop it, you have to run to the wall and say 'Suicide!' before someone else picks up the ball and hits you with it, or the Mongooses swing out of the trees and slit your throat with Clip's knife. If you're hit, you're out and have to sit off in the grass at the edge of the lot."

We turn to the Wall to play, but the Chief says there's something else. "The moms. They're coming to get you."

We thought we had more time. We haven't learned to fight, though I can jam the chair under the bathroom doorknob. I haven't even had my man's period even though I've been naked in front of women. We play with the Chief through dinner, unsure what else there really is. He picks up the rules pretty fast.

Warren hears it first and stops the game. He holds the ball and says, "Listen!" A sound like bells is coming out of the neighborhood, and I think at first that it's the bats. But as the noise gets louder, we realize what we're hearing. Every phone in the neighborhood is ringing.

"That's it," the Chief says. "It's all over. They're getting ready. This will be the night."

Roger and the Mongooses come out of the trees with all their heads cocked to the noise. Clip flinches and scrambles to his feet and stands behind Milk and Eric. He has cut himself again and is bleeding.

"What's happening?" Roger asks. We tell him. The Mongooses look scared and then all the ringing stops. I show them the tennis balls in the trash can. The Mongooses have a few of the archery sets they stole from the camp and some big red balls for kickball.

Mom is coming. All the moms are coming, every one in the neighborhood. A line of light blue cars appears on the street, all with their orange turn signals flashing, and they all pull in the driveway to the Arboretum. We see our dads sitting in the passenger seats, looking like we do when we get driven to school. Lovely and Dr. Hesterwill sit in the back seat of my car. Our dads get out first and sit on the grass at the edge of the lot, just watching to see how this will go, never really looking at us. Then the moms slam all their doors, and we see they have their phones with them. We make the sign and hiss.

The moms step onto the lot, and the Mongooses pull back the arrows in their bows, waiting for Roger to say when. Chief Big Homo — Edward — grips a kickball to punt. The dads hold their breath and hug themselves on the grass at the edge of the lot, mine shuffling through his cards but not looking at any of them. Then there's a ringing, maybe from the bats, and the moms charge with their phones up in the air, and we Rattlesnakes let fly with the tennis balls like the stars finally fell out of the sky.

Saint Kevin of Fox Chase

THE NIGHT KEVIN WAS killed, I was out there running, too. For weeks, he had been trying to convince Clip and me to hang out at the Fox Chase playground on Friday nights. The older kids were buying beer and selling cups for a buck. The girls who came were getting wild, dancing to the music blasting out of car stereos and flashing their chests at the boys.

I was skeptical. The guys who hung around the playground at night were not my friends; they were bad news, got in fights, smoked. I knew some of them from soccer, and we had a tenuous truce because I could play. But I didn't want to tempt things, and didn't care too much about drinking beer. Seventh grade is a tenuous time.

Usually, Clip and I spent our Friday nights drinking black cherry soda and making prank phone calls. Sometimes my sister, Lovely, and her friends would be camped out in the basement, and we would hover on the landing, hoping to hear something about sex. At the time, we were both desperate to get blow jobs, and while technically we knew what sexual act was being referred to, we were curious about the name. It was the word "blow" that was confusing us the most.

Kevin finally convinced us to go to the playground by invoking that mysterious word, saying, "Milk and Eric both got blow-jobbed this weekend, and the girl wants to give more." The word "give" was also strange to me. A person "had" sex, "made" love, but this was something that could only be given. It sounded special.

"Who is this girl?" Clip asked, as if it mattered. "Some pig?"

"No, no. She's hot. Lives out of the parish. Just come."

Clip and I talked it over on the walk home from school that Monday afternoon.

"I've got five bucks," he said. "That's five beers. Is that enough?"

I shrugged.

"How much are you gonna bring?"

"I've got ten bucks. I could get more if I tell Mom and Dad I'm doing something else."

"Do we have to pay that girl? I don't want to do that."

"Doesn't sound like it. She's giving them away."

We talked so ridiculously about sex back then, probably because we thought about it all the time, privately, and with little insight. Catholic school, in its attempts to inspire abstinence, had filled us instead with a strange, superstitious brand of horniness. The myth of the Catholic schoolgirl—this was surely started by kids just like Clip and me.

Our ignorance about this subject was something we only spoke about late on weekend nights when Clip slept over and we clicked through cable to find some movie with sex in it. Clip had brought it up just a week before.

"Hey, so does the girl, like, actually *blow* on it?" he had said.

I was relieved because I thought I was the only one who didn't know.

"I don't know," I had admitted. "What's a 'dildo'?"

"I know that one. It's a plastic dick girls use."

"Weird. Where do they buy one?"

"No idea. So what's a 'cervix'? My aunt had cancer there."

"I don't know, but I know it has a hood."

"A hood?" Clip had thought this was hysterical. "In case it rains?"

I laughed, too. At times, it felt like I wanted to understand a woman's body more than I wanted to touch one, scared of the school yard quizzes and dares. But sometimes, the degree of our ignorance was just funny.

"I don't know why," I tried to tell him. "It was in the book." The same book he had at home. The same book the nuns gave the boys the day they gave the girls tampons.

Clip started to sing. "Rain, rain, go away! My cervix wears a hood!"

I gagged on black cherry soda, and Clip kept singing, holding a blanket over his head, until finally Dad thumped on the floor above us to keep it down. We shushed and wiped our eyes.

"Weird," Clip said.

"Yeah, weird."

So by the time we parted ways on Strahle Street that Monday afternoon—he to cross Pine Road and me to go down the hill at Ryers—we had agreed that we'd go to the playground on Friday night.

Back then, I was the fastest kid in Philadelphia. Not in a track-meet way—nothing was official—but I could chase down any kid, given enough room to run. This mainly happened on the soccer field where I played sweeper, the last line of defense, and I was known—feared, I imagined—in all the other neighborhoods for catching every breakaway winger who crossed the fifty-yard line.

No one ever expected it. I was bone-skinny, almost lost inside my huge red-and-black uniform, and had thick glasses strapped to my head. They never heard me coming, and were shocked to find me in front of them suddenly—between them and the goal—and taking the ball away from them. Running was something almost spiritual for me then. Once I found my rhythm, the rest of the world was beaten off as my heart and lungs and legs synched up into a state close to hypnosis. It was joy.

And we were a good team. We'd won the city's Department of Recreation championship the year before and had jackets made with our numbers and positions stitched on them. We strutted around school like a gang.

Kevin was a small, stocky kid, but a fearless goalie. He was often out of position, but threw himself recklessly at the ball. He tangled himself in the net, slammed into the goalposts, but kept the ball out and could punt that thing well across midfield. He was a talker back there, too, always yelling at the rest of us since he had the best view of the field. "Who's got fourteen? Pick up fourteen!"

Clip was center halfback, the workhorse on the field. He ran the field between the eighteen-yard lines and was never more than ten yards away from the ball. He threw up on the field from exhaustion a lot—water and orange rinds splashing in the grass.

But the game was changing.

At twelve, I was still ignored by puberty while my teammates and opponents were growing legs like tree trunks, lifting weights, shaving. When we were younger, soccer was mainly a game of kick-and-chase, but that season it became brutal. It was no longer about who was lucky enough to be near the goal as the ball pinballed around the field, but rather who could knock his opponents out of the play. There were lots of penalty cards, a fight every other game, and vicious, sailor-like cursing on the field. The parents became more aggressive, too, feeding off of the violence of their kids. Fathers fought in the parking lot after the game; mothers screeched from the sidelines. My own dad was thrown out of a game once for threatening the referee.

Given our success the season before, we moved to a different league and began playing the tougher neighborhoods in the city. I had never been to any of these strange places before, and even their names were frightening to me: Kensington, Port Richmond, Frankford. They sounded more like the names of World War II battles than playgrounds. Driving with my father to these games, I was always quiet and nervous, looking at the run-down neighborhoods where our opponents were from, imagining them to be monsters—not kids—raised in such blight: barred windows; packs of men wandering the streets, yelling at cars; pigeons drinking brown rainwater off of the pavement.

On Wednesday night of the week Kevin was killed, we had our first playoff game in Fishtown. Night games in the bad neighborhoods were the worst. Most of the parents on the opposing team would be drunk, and many of the spectators weren't even parents, just bums from the block, wandering around, stopping to watch and yell.

The field at Fishtown was made of gravel and speckled with glass. It sparkled under the lights like the surface of the moon. We had never seen anything like this. Many of the city fields were uneven and scrappy, or ran up and down hills, or even held pitcher's mounds in their boundaries for the spring, but they were still made of grass. During warm-ups, some chatter started among us that we should refuse to play because of the conditions. But Coach reprimanded us, while scratching aggressively at his crotch, that that was exactly the reaction these thugs expected from us and we were tougher than that. None of us believed it. So we took the field reluctantly, feeling too fancy in our bright red uniforms and new cleats.

The Fishtown kids were ugly. They had their soccer numbers shaved into the backs of their heads. Their uniforms were a washed-out bluish-gray, and it was clear they had been handed down. Two kids on the team wore the number ten, surely a Department of Recreation violation. We tried to bring this to the ref's attention, with no luck. At this level, most refs were just local kids, and he assured us he knew the difference between the two number tens. Before the game, the ref hung around on the Fishtown sidelines, shaking hands and kissing babies.

It was a rout. The Fishtown kids knew how to negotiate the cinder field while we fell and bled. The rocks were like quicksand, trapping our expensive shoes and smothering our pansy ideas about rules. I chased some kids down, but had my legs kicked out from under me whenever I did, no whistle. My knees were covered in glass by halftime, and Kevin's hands were bloody from diving into the gravel. When Coach tried to talk to the ref about the calls he was missing, the Fishtown parents started yelling curses across the field. Our sidelines were quiet.

Fed up, Kevin started mouthing off between the goalposts. The Fishtown kids were shoving him out of position and kicking him after he had picked up the ball—fouls on any other field.

"Hey, number eight!" he was yelling. "Kick me again. See what happens!"

Number eight was a snaggletoothed kid a head taller than Kevin. Eight looked at me. He wore regular tube socks with strapless shin pads stuffed underneath that had slid around to the back of his leg. Blood and something else black stained the front of his socks, maybe old blood.

"You want something?" he asked between gulps of air. If he had taken out a cigarette right there on the field, I wouldn't have been surprised.

I stood between him and Kevin with my hands on my hips and shook my head.

"I'll kick what I want," he told us.

We were inside the six-yard line, waiting for a corner kick. No one else heard what was going on. The ref hadn't blown the whistle yet.

Kevin got furious. "Kick my ass then! I'll knock you out on this piece-of-shit field!"

The ref finally came bounding in with his yellow card for Kevin, but the fight had already broken out. Kevin swung a short arm that only caught Eight in the side. Eight grabbed his arm, threw Kevin onto the ground, and dived down into his chest and stomach with punches. Kevin's mom was howling from the sidelines, and I couldn't tell whether she was urging him on or screaming at him to stop. I went cold with fear, expecting to get hit any minute, but nothing happened. I bent down to retie my shoes, like I didn't know what was happening.

The ref finally pulled Eight off of Kevin, and the rest of the Fishtown kids were laughing. They had seen better fights, was what their smiles seemed to be saying.

Kevin was crying as the ref walked him over to the sidelines. Our backup goalie, C.J. — who had been practicing head balls with someone's little brother twenty yards off the field and who had no idea what had just happened or even that the field was not grass at all but rocks and glass—edged his way onto the field, not looking too happy. He strapped his expensive goalie gloves on and stood in front of the net as if it were about to trap him.

For all intents and purposes, we stopped playing. We'd chase and poke at the ball, but avoided any contact. They fired shot after shot at poor C.J., and it seemed as if they had more players on the field than we did.

Finally, the ref blew the whistle to end the game. We lost 7–0 and our season was over.

On the long ride home, back through that awful neighborhood and up onto 95, I could tell Dad was mad. Usually, we talked about the game, the big plays, the big mistakes, and mainly my own performance. That night, Dad was quiet.

I wanted to tell him that I wanted to fight, too, but he would have known that was a lie. Instead, he wove through four lanes of traffic, and I wondered if I would ever learn to drive like this—to maneuver the car between gears using both feet, to know the best way to get to every neighborhood in the city the way he seemed to, to fly between tractor-trailers at 70 mph without crashing.

As we got off the expressway, Dad finally spoke.

"This guy in my unit at work dropped his pants in the lobby of our building this morning. I'm going to have to fire him."

He barely ever talked to me about work. He worked for the city in the Department of Revenue, making sure people paid what they owed, occasionally making jokes at restaurants or departments stores, when my family didn't get the service he expected, that he would audit them. So I wanted to say something, especially since it wasn't about the game. And I was afraid I was being audited in his mind. I felt delinquent in something; a debt had been accrued that night I only partially understood.

"Is he crazy?" I asked.

"Yeah," he said, "crazy," as if that were beside the point.

"Is he a good worker?" I wasn't sure whether Dad was disappointed or entertained by this news about his employee.

"No, of course not. He wants to get fired."

Hearing about adults acting this way always amazed me. I always assumed at some point I would know all the answers. A switch would be flipped and I'd be grown up. But every once in a while there was proof that no one had it figured out, that the bungling of childhood could persist and get further out of hand as the years went by.

"The thing is," Dad continued, "this guy, Gorham, is not the worst of the bunch. When he's not drinking and he takes his medicine, he's okay. I mean, for instance, Walsh's mom calls me once a week to say I'm being mean to her son at work. He's forty-seven. See what I mean?"

"What do you say when she calls?" I was thinking Mom had made plenty of calls on my behalf.

"I tell her I'm busy. I tell her he's an adult who can solve his own problems." Dad sped through a yellow light and dropped the car down the hill through Pennypack Park. The trees covered us, and he kept talking. "But it's not true. He's a forty-seven-year-old kid. He *asks* his mom to call."

At that moment, Dad seemed almost desperate enough to ask me for advice. But the question never came; he changed the subject.

"How about old C.J. tonight? He looked like he was at the wrong end of a firing squad." He paused, but I knew what was next. "No thanks to you. You guys sure left Kevin high and dry."

Dad and I rolled through more familiar neighborhoods, getting closer to home. Somehow the buildings seemed friendlier; the harsh light of the lampposts took on a warm orange glow. Here was Roosevelt Mall; here was the street you turned down to get to Clip's house; and here was our playground, still lit up this late at night, its grass a bright, healthy green under gigantic floodlights. That awful field of rocks and glass, the screaming parents, the fight—all of that started to seem like a bad dream, something that would hopefully make no sense in the morning

At home, Mom fussed over my cut-up knees. I tried to ignore them, but they did burn. The blood had blackened around bits of lodged green and brown glass into a strange sort of mosaic. She was horrified when I described the awful field, but Dad just shook his head.

"Well, how'd you do?" she asked, getting a wet washrag and the bottle of peroxide.

"We got killed," I said.

Mom looked at Dad to hear his side.

"Yup," he said. "Killed."

Neither of us said anything about the fight. She pressed the rag to my knee, and I winced at the sting.

"Well, that doesn't seem fair, to have to play on a field like that," Mom said.

I looked up at Dad.

"There's nothing to do about it. It's the playoffs."

"It just doesn't seem right. Someone is going to get hurt. If they get cut on that glass . . ."

I was nodding along with Mom, but said nothing. Dad shook his head again and walked into the bathroom, where he tuned his old radio and began to shave. The hot water poured into the sink, and the steam crept through the cracks of the door toward Mom and me. The radio had been his father's and had a leather strap attached to it as if you would carry it around, heavy as it was. I knew he was trying to find the Flyers' game that had just started on the West Coast, but all he could pick up was music, tinny and simple, and screeching from those old, blown speakers.

Thursday morning at school, word spread quickly about Kevin's fight. His eye was swollen a little. If it had been me, I would have used it as an excuse to stay home from school, but then I saw the wisdom in Kevin's decision. The girls in our class were especially interested and wanted to hear about the game, play by play. I tried to show off my mangled knee, but I couldn't get my starchy uniform pants up that high. Instead, I faked a limp.

Kevin talked about the fight nonchalantly, as if it were something that just had to happen. Friday night was still on his mind. He grabbed me and Clip as our class walked to singing practice in the church.

"You guys are still coming tomorrow night, right?"

Clip and I looked at each other, waiting for the other to speak.

"How much money should we bring?" Clip asked finally. He was obsessed with this aspect of the adventure for some reason.

"It doesn't matter," Kevin told him. He looked at me. "What's his problem?"

I shrugged and wondered if Kevin was scared, too. He wanted so desperately for us to go.

Our church was a tan brick building lined with stained-glass saints. A stone statue of our patroness, Saint Cecilia, stood holding a harp above the steps to the entrance. The parishioners in Fox Chase were of the new breed of harmless Irish Catholics. They went to church once a week out of habit more than anything else, prayed for a short homily from the priest, but brought their kids and gave ten dollars a week to the collection. As such, the church was large and well kept. Marble steps, elaborate flower arrangements, and new vestments for the priests and altar boys every year.

Sister Thomas grimaced at my class as we filed into the pews—the boys sliding on the polished wood, the girls crowded in a constant whisper. The nun cleared her throat repeatedly, attempting to silence us without screaming in God's house. She had achieved the goal of her order—she was truly a sexless creature. Not a wisp of hair stuck out from beneath her habit, and if it weren't for the fact that her uniform bottomed out into something like a dress, she would have been unidentifiable as a woman. Her fat face was pinched into a permanent, righteous scowl that killed any more speculation about blow jobs in my mind for the time being.

Weeks earlier, she had smiled when she explained to our class that she was married to Christ, but we knew it was really us she was bound to. She was from that lost generation who had been admired when they first entered the convent at eighteen, but now most respect for the vocation had evaporated and she was left married to a ghost.

Ms. Gergen perched behind the organ, waiting for the signal from Sister Thomas. She seemed to us only slightly more of a woman than the nun. Under the lights in the church, her scalp was visible through her thin hair. Her voice was nice enough—just a notch below operatic—but when coupled with our own pubescent ones, we made each other sound ridiculous.

"Louder, louder!" Sister Thomas screeched above the din of our singing. Clip and I smiled at each other and filled our lungs.

"We are many parts!" we crooned flatly. "We are all one body!"—though Clip sang "cervix" in the place of "body" and we cracked up. By the end of every practice, the students would all be screaming—actually having fun—but nowhere near the right notes. For some reason, Sister Thomas seemed satisfied with this result, though we usually scared away the parishioners who were praying in the back.

"Remember," Sister Thomas said as practice ended, "Saint Cecilia is the patron saint of music. Let's do her proud at Mass tomorrow."

Clip leaned in. "She also had her head cut off."

This wasn't exactly true, but Saint Cecilia was a martyr. She had been a virgin, like us, and refused her pagan husband on their wedding night, saying she was already bound to an angel. When the news got around that Cecilia had converted her new husband and his buddies into Christians, the Romans finally came after her. Her executioners chopped at her neck three times before they gave up and left her to die. She bled for three days—her head still basically attached—and performed miracles in her home.

We always liked stories like this where the church seemed wild and action-packed, completely different from our lives on the parish playground and at Sunday Mass. And while we were attracted to the violence and gore of this particular story, we had no idea what any of that had to do with music. It was one of the many simple questions the nuns could never answer for us: Why should we sing louder for this woman? What is the connection between murder and music?

The answer, I've learned, is not as interesting as the question. A botched Latin translation, a few misinformed painters, the signature of a medieval pope, and Saint Cecilia is now never seen away from her organ or harp. She is not the patron saint of, as Clip suggested many times, laryngitis or neck pain, but instead her legacy of strength, certainly—and horror as well—grew into something calm and beautiful, though maybe wrong.

And so, Kevin.

On Friday night, Clip and I walked to the playground. He brought his soccer ball, and we passed it back and forth across the width of the street as we walked. It was eight o'clock, but dark as midnight.

"Think you're going to try out for the high school team next year?" Clip asked.

"Probably," I said, but I had already made up my mind that I wouldn't.

Clip dug his toe under the ball and lifted it across the street. I trapped it perfectly under my foot and kept walking. Coach had told us to never be away from a ball, to kick it everywhere, sleep with it, know every bounce it could possibly take. His advice worked. Clip and I could pass the ball all night between us without even thinking or ever having to chase it down. I could put that ball in Clip's pocket if I wanted to.

The lights of the playground rose above the row homes as we got closer, as if God himself were turning a crank and raising our destiny. We slowed our pace a little.

"I say we check it out, see what's going on," Clip said. "But I bet there's no girls. No beer."

"Probably not. Kevin's full of shit."

We walked through the parking lot at Saint Cecilia's, and our saint, lit from below, was looking old and unmusical. Memory now puts a frown on her face, twists it into Sister Thomas's, my mother's, my sister's even, saying, *Don't go.* But instead we smirked at her, thinking of singing practice, and Clip started again with his own lyrics, "I am many parts! She is all one body! And the gifts we have! We are given to share!" He thrust his hips out with each downbeat of the song. Had she not been stone, our saint maybe would have shaken her head at us, knowing we were scared but too cocky to ask for help. She had been neither.

Clip pointed to the rectory and the convent, the home of the parish's priests and nuns, our conscience. "Think they'll come over and break it up?"

"Nah," I said, "They can't see anything. That tree's in the way." This was true: a large dogwood grew in front of the convent door, and the rectory's view of the playground was blocked by the church.

As we crossed Rhawn Street toward the playground, a carload of kids sped past and screamed, "Fags!" Clip gave them the finger, and I wished that he hadn't.

Walking up the driveway, I could see a crowd on the basketball court, but in the dark I couldn't make out any of their faces, just the orange tips of cigarettes and the flash of red Dixie cups. I tried to walk like I belonged there, like I was a regular in the Friday crowd, whatever that might look like. Clip picked up his ball.

The kids stared back at us, eyes hidden under low baseball caps and hoods. They stopped talking as we approached, and there was a tense moment before Kevin finally burst from the crowd toward us.

"Hey, you fags came!"

Clip looked at me and raised his eyebrows. I was unsettled at being called that name twice already tonight.

"Get a beer," Kevin said and pointed to a green Explorer with its trunk open.

We walked over and a kid with a goatee said, "A buck for the cup. A buck for the beer."

I gave him a five, and he handed me a cup, saying, "I don't got change."

"Okay," I said, "I'll buy his, too."

The kid with the goatee chuckled. "You two on a date?"

A group of girls I had never seen before stood nearby, most wearing high school jackets from different parishes. They were staring at us. I suddenly felt silly in my soccer jacket. It was just a kid's game and we weren't even the champs anymore. I noticed Kevin wasn't wearing his, but he bounced comfortably between packs of kids I didn't know. Finally, he came back to Clip and me.

"See that girl over there in the Saint Hubert's jacket?" he asked and poked Clip in the chest. "She likes you."

The girl in question had long blond hair, frosted and crimped. She lit a cigarette. She was somewhat pretty, though not the prettiest of the bunch, and maybe even a little taller than Clip. He took a big, ambitious mouthful of his beer—his first beer ever.

"So what do I do?" he finally asked, looking back over his shoulder toward the traffic on Rhawn Street, away from the party, as if only half interested. The group of girls was staring and giggling.

These were not the girls of Saint Cecilia's Elementary. Where was freckled Erin McManus, or cute and chubby Anne Marie Gerelli with the slight mustache, or even poor Cathy Ranster, who still had to go to speech therapy to say her r's right? Those girls I could handle. I could even flirt with them in a limp, seventh-grade kind of way. This was different.

"Go talk to her!" Kevin said. "Ask her to take a walk. Do *something*."

Then Clip did something amazing. Something that may have even saved his life that night. He suddenly adjusted his head and his grip on his beer, and walked over to that crowd of girls. Kevin and I were shocked. We watched as if waiting for an anvil to fall on him at any minute, but nothing happened.

He made the long journey across the basketball court, crossed line after line, and began to speak.

My beer was going flat in my hand. The foam had bubbled off, and I realized that I had gotten only half a cupful for my dollar. I didn't care.

Now Kevin turned to me. "There might be some trouble tonight," he said. "You down to fight?"

"Trouble?" I asked as I took a sip of beer. I was expecting at any moment to be drunk, having no idea how much or how long it took.

"Yeah, some girl from Abington is saying Roger raped her up here last Friday. And someone said they saw a car of Abington kids riding around the neighborhood earlier. It's probably nothing, but—"

He dug in his pocket and pulled out a black goalie glove with quarters duct-taped to the knuckles.

"What is that?" I asked.

"Just in case." He put it on and pretended to punch me in the jaw. This was ridiculous. "Rape" was a word I'd only heard spoken on the news. And Roger was just another skinny kid like me, but with black hair hanging into his eyes. Was he capable of something like this? Would he even know how to do it if he wanted to? All signs pointed to "no." I scanned the crowd and found him finally, standing between two parked cars, holding a beer, his eyes shifting back and forth and his face more serious than I'd ever seen it. I waved to him, but he didn't look at me.

Kevin was calm. He pointed to the pack of strange girls, whose numbers were thinning out as the night wore on. "So are you gonna talk to someone, or just get drunk?"

Clip and his girl had disappeared, though his soccer ball was resting right there on the playground's concrete, begging to be kicked. Perhaps, I thought, he was being given a blow job, and all I could picture was a good-size present wrapped in a big bow being handed over by a Christmas elf.

I finished my beer and bought another from the snickering kid with the goatee. Then Kevin pulled me over to the girls. I took my glasses off as if I only wore them at times that necessitated great scrutiny. I tried to appear relaxed, but the girls were now just a blurry net of frizzy hair. I thought there might be either three or four of them. A voice spoke up, and I tried to rely on my ears for guidance.

"You play soccer?" one of them said.

"Yeah," I replied, and took another sip of my beer. I was desperate to say more, could feel Kevin's eyes boring into me, like, *Now's your chance!*—but all I could come up with was "Do you?"

The girls giggled. I felt silly, but it was not a ridiculous question. Allison Michener, in my grade, was getting a scholarship to high school for soccer. Plenty of girls played.

"No," the same girl's voice replied. "Are you any good?"

"I'm okay," I said, but Kevin stuck up for me.

"City All Star two years in a row!" He punched me in the arm.

The girls murmured a little, not much impressed. Finally, one of them spoke up. "Can I try on your glasses?"

Anyone who wears glasses knows this is always a bad thing to do. You are completely at the mercy of the borrower, and your blind litany of "c'mon, give them back, c'mon" never works as fast as you'd like. But she touched my arm and I handed them over.

"Wow! You're blind!"

She passed them to the girl next to her while I dumbly held my hand out, hoping to get them back soon. Kevin disappeared.

"So are you here for the fight?" the first girl asked.

"No. I'm just hanging out," I said, getting more nervous about what was going to happen that night.

"Good. I don't like fighting. It's stupid."

I nodded. She was right, though I wondered if something else was being said beneath the surface that I didn't quite understand.

"Well, you want to take a walk, Four-Eyes?"

"Sure," I said, and she took my arm. Up close, I could tell she had gotten my glasses back from her friends, but I knew I couldn't walk for long without them. She pulled me away from the group, the other girls still giggling, and I was thinking, *This is it! Clip and me on the same night!*, when, because I was so blind, it suddenly looked like a fleet of 747s was landing in the playground parking lot. The halos around the headlights of the cars were huge, and the noise of the engines and the screeching of tires suggested something awful had just arrived.

I snatched at my glasses, and the girl let me take them back, herself mesmerized by these new arrivals.

"We should get out of here," she said.

Kids were piling out of four cars like clowns, and the older guys from our playground approached them, cursing and telling them to get out. The girl pulled me harder, back toward the soccer fields. When I looked back, I saw one of the kids pull a baseball bat out and smash one of our guys' headlights. Out of habit, I picked up Clip's soccer ball—an Adidas Tango, hand-stitched, a Christmas present, the envy of any field. Even fully inflated, the ball was soft in my arms, and I held it to my chest until the girl took my hand.

"Run," the girl said, and I did.

We found out later that these kids *were* from Abington, a neighborhood just outside of the city, five minutes away. These were suburban kids, not the glass-eating monsters of Fishtown or the barbed-wire thugs of Kensington. Their parents were doctors and private school teachers. Audis, in-ground pools, ski trips. According to dumb neighborhood logic, we should have been tougher than them, crashing *their* playground. But at the time, racing across that field in the dark, they seemed like Romans with torches. Like demons.

I have always played defense, scored only once or twice, and then by accident. In soccer, defense meant chasing people, a ball, a thing. No one chases the sweeper. There's no point. Now, I was on the defensive that night, to be sure, but lost with no object to run down or goal to protect. The girl had to pull on my arm to keep me on track while I veered all over the field. *So this is what it's like,* I thought. I was the breakaway winger hearing something like me but worse breathing down his neck.

The girl knew what she was doing. The back end of the playground emptied out through the trees onto Ridgeway Street. When we hit the street, the girl grabbed me and pulled me down between two parked cars.

"I live right over there. Where do you?"

I explained it was a good fifteen-minute walk.

"Don't go straight home," she told me. "Stay on big streets as much as you can and hide if a car rides by." It was good advice, and I wondered how many times she had done this. A car rumbled past and we froze. "Okay, Four-Eyes. Get home. Be careful." She kissed my cheek and disappeared down the street.

I was ten blocks from home with the fight in between. I had lost Clip and was wearing a jacket that identified me as a target. My neighborhood had become evil in a matter of minutes, and I was drunk for the first time and lost in it.

I knew Ridgeway hit Rhawn Street at an angle, about a block away from the church, very close to the playground. Or I could walk out of my way toward the train tracks and follow them home, but risk a run-in with a different type of thug—the drug kids and the skateboarders, the tenth-grade Satan worshippers. I didn't want that either. Or I could just wait there behind the lines and hope the fight didn't come to me. This was cowardly but, like most things cowardly, safe.

In the end, I didn't have a choice. After five minutes of waiting, a car came up from behind and slowed down as it approached me. I started walking, Clip's ball under my arm, and tried to pretend I had just come from practice. The beer in my stomach began to churn.

They started yelling from the car, "Hey! Hey, kid, where are you going? Hey, Fox Chase!"

I looked up the street. There were no other cars coming that might save me. But I couldn't be alone. Ridgeway was lined with row homes on the other side of the street. I ran to the first door I could reach and banged on it. The Abington kids, about twenty feet farther down the street, put on their flashers and popped the trunk. A kid got out, his eye on me the whole time, and pretended to be looking for something in the back. Finally, the door opened.

A man in a white undershirt with yellowed armpits stood glaring at me. A small, angry dog yapped from behind him.

"Shut up!" he said and turned to me. "What?"

"Please," I said, "I'm in trouble. I need to use the phone. Can I please come in?"

"More of you hoodlums? Always pissing on my grass or keying my car! Get out of here before I call the cops."

"Please call them. There's bad—" But by then, he had shut the door. Inside, the dog kept barking and I could hear a woman say, "Who was that?"

I found out later, this happened all over the neighborhood that night. Grown men slamming doors in kids' faces, some of them streaked with blood. I wasn't the only one who thought I could retreat back to the world of adults for safety. And I wasn't the only one denied access, having come this far, just wanting blow jobs and beer. It wasn't until two or three of us kids banged on the same door, or words like "kill" or "murder" were used, that the parents finally called the cops. And they did it reluctantly, embarrassed, maybe even a little ashamed, saying things like, *I know this sounds crazy and I hate to bother you but* . . . I know because they played the tapes on TV weeks later. On the other end, the cops must have taken it the same way. *Probably nothing, a spooked housewife, drunk kids causing trouble. It's a good neighborhood.*

But I was fast. My pursuers were obviously drunker than me and did not know the neighborhood. But none of this information seemed available to me as I launched myself off of the row home's steps and headed back toward the playground. The beer mixed with adrenaline, and their shouts got louder and more ferocious. I cut through the trees back up onto the soccer fields, thinking I could lose them in the open stretches.

By now, the timer on the playground's lights had rendered the field completely dark. Two hundred yards off, the basketball court was lit up only by a few headlights, but I had no idea whether they were friendly or not. So I ran to the opposite side of the field, also lined with trees, and hid in the pitch-dark. I watched my pursuers slow to a stop. I could tell from their silhouettes that they were carrying weapons—more bats, it looked like. Finally, they turned around and went back the way we came, presumably to get back in the car.

I panted in the dark, unsure of whether I could make another run like that if I had to. Then I threw up.

I wasn't the first person to find Kevin. When all the cars finally left the basketball court, I walked across the field toward

Rhawn Street. The neighborhood was quiet. The church was still lit up, and the floodlights shining up on the statue of Saint Cecilia were throwing giant shadows across the building's front. People were milling around out front—two girls, it looked like—and as I crossed the street, they screamed at me, "Get away! Get the fuck outta here!" Between the two girls, a figure lay crumpled on the asphalt.

This was Kevin. Recognizable now only by his clothes, his head—beaten with baseball bats—made a strange, unnatural silhouette against the concrete. The girls circled him like wild animals, and I kept my distance.

"The cops are coming! You're in deep shit!" they were yelling.

I recognized one of the girls from the basketball court earlier that night, but obviously they didn't know me. The girls finally quieted down, pacing around and stooping over Kevin. I hung around the edges of the scene and wondered if the church was open this late at night. No, it wouldn't be. They stopped doing that years ago, I remembered.

Two cop cars pulled up, and the girls started screaming again.

"An ambulance! We need an ambulance!"

A few nuns came out of the convent and quickly blessed themselves when they saw the scene. Sister Thomas, in a green sweat suit and with a head of short brown hair, tried to usher the girls away, and their piety resurfaced out of habit. Their ferocious cursing stopped.

"Sister, no, he's dying! Please help!"

Sister Thomas, stripped of her uniform now, seemed like a real person to me for the first time. She hugged the girls and began to sob, recognizing Kevin as one of hers. But not hers. Could it be the whole celibate life came crashing down on her, the love for children she had no authority over? Who hated her, though she stayed awake at night worrying about them?

Worrying about something just like this? My thoughts about these people are confused. And if things were reversed, if it were Sister Thomas dying here on the steps of this church, would Kevin, or any of us, have cared?

The ambulance pulled up, and then two priests came out of the rectory. One opened the church with an elaborate set of keys and turned on all its lights. A crowd was starting to gather—more nuns and priests, panting kids like me, a few parents even. The paramedics looked at Kevin quickly and scooped him up on a stretcher. They said nothing to the crowd before they sped off.

I got closer now, emboldened by the crowd, and heard every conversation: the small nun asking the cops if she could clean up Kevin's blood; a mother and father grabbing someone else's kid, demanding to know where their son was; two priests saying to each other, yes, a prayer, but which one?

Probably, around that time, someone had the awful job of calling Kevin's parents.

Father Fitz stopped me and asked what happened.

"A fight," I told him.

"This was no fight." He toed the concrete with a pair of running shoes; he wasn't wearing his collar either. "Help me get everyone inside the church."

I nodded, but he did all the talking. I wandered among the crowd, numb and confident since I knew what had happened and finally felt somewhat safe. Eventually, everyone filed into the foyer, eyes stinging with tears and desperately trying to adjust to the harsh lights of the church.

"We should say a prayer now. For Kevin. For all of us. Heavenly Father," he started, "have mercy on us all. Saint Cecilia, give your parish strength . . ." Everyone bowed their heads, but it seemed mainly out of exhaustion and shame.

· · ·

I walked to Clip's house. I wasn't scared anymore. I felt for some naive reason that nothing worse could happen that night, like some sort of quota had been filled. I imagined I could hear the engines of Abington cars speeding home, expelled from the parish by our priests and nuns like an exorcism. When I got to Clip's, he was outside on his stoop with a big grin. I threw him his soccer ball.

"You won't believe what happened!" he said.

"They killed Kevin."

"What are you talking about?"

"Those kids. With cars and baseball bats."

"He's dead? What kids?"

I shrugged. Clip stood up and bounced the ball once.

"Where were you?" I asked finally.

"I went to that girl's car. Then she drove me back. Her name's Michelle."

"Did something happen?"

He nodded, the grin creeping back.

What was this? That night, Clip had been saved by horniness and driven home by a beautiful girl while the rest of us ran for our lives. And Kevin had been killed playing host and protector of our neighborhood. I thought of Saint Cecilia, though I wouldn't be the only one to do that over the next few months.

I wasn't mad at Clip, but I couldn't talk to him then. He could tell me what a blow job was like later, and I'd tell him what a dead body looked like.

When I got home, my mom was on the phone and quickly hung up when she saw me.

"Are you okay? Something's happened to Kevin."

"I know," I said.

"What? How?"

"I saw him."

. . .

By Saturday afternoon, Fox Chase was aflame with rumors and accusations. A neighbor, Mr. Kramer, told my dad and me he just knew it was the blacks who did this, and when I began to tell him, no, it was just white kids like me and his own two sons—I saw them—my dad shushed me. Then Kramer told us he's moving to the suburbs as soon as he can, "where it's safe." The cops were blamed for not responding fast enough. Even the poor priests and nuns got their share of abuse since Kevin was killed on their property, practically on the church steps.

When someone was brave enough to suggest that maybe kids shouldn't be out late on Fridays drinking and getting into fights, she was shouted down quickly by the neighborhood fathers. "I did the same thing when I was a kid, and I turned out fine. Boys will be . . ."

Parents were interviewed on the news; they pushed their way on camera. Everyone suddenly knew Kevin. Claimed to know what their kids did, and to know that their kids were completely different from Kevin's attackers. There was no mention of Kevin's glove. Or the weapons our own guys had but were too startled to reach.

A week later, while Kevin was being proclaimed the martyr of the neighborhood, Dad finally talked to me about Kevin's death. The wooden fence in our backyard had collapsed, and I held the posts while he nailed them back together.

"What happened that night?" he asked, fishing through his tool belt for a nail.

I told him everything. I told him about the beer and the girls and the running across the field. The bats and the blood and the prayers. It was a confession. And I was ashamed again, as if describing a bad soccer game but worse. So many times before, Dad had told me how I had let our goalie—Kevin—down. And here it was, the big failure I had been training for.

Dad stopped hammering. "You know what the problem is?"

He stepped away from the fence and ran his hands over his face, pulling his skin tight over the bone, erasing the years and bullshit that had harrowed him. He looked young for a second, and the fence sagged as he let it go. On the other side was just a mirror image of our own small backyard.

I didn't answer the question, and neither did he. Instead, he grabbed me by the shoulders. "Look. Run from idiots, you hear me? Run from thugs. Run from liars. You're fast. You can."

He went inside and I heard the sink start to gush. I thought for a second that I might fix the fence myself, but Dad had taken the tools with him.

The details of Kevin's death came out eventually. Stories were patched together. Probably twenty other kids had stories like mine, kids who saw Kevin and then lost him, everyone running for their lives without knowing it, making choices in the heat of the moment that decided everything.

But the best report was from Roger, the unapologetic cause of it all. He had run across the busy traffic of Rhawn Street with Kevin toward the church and school to get away from the kids with bats. But in the parking lot, Kevin finally stopped to fight. It was what a good goalie does. Turning on his pursuers, he must have realized his mistake as four kids, two with baseball bats, charged even harder. Roger watched from fifty feet off, not stopping when Kevin did, and no doubt confused why his friend had made that decision or what to do next. According to Roger, he saw Kevin get hit in the side with a bat and then run stupidly, confused by pain, back toward the playground.

Roger ran home at this point, told his parents nothing, probably swore into his pillow over and over that, of course, he never raped anyone. But we know that this was when Kevin was killed. On a busy street, under our saint, traffic whizzing past the frenzy, headlights aiming straight ahead. Some of the other kids limped around after that night, eyes shining black around their edges; they had fought a little and run, but these were not trophies anymore.

Mass was crowded in those weeks after Kevin's death. The congregation always comes back in tragedy, the same way that the neighborhood bars were probably also filled. But Father Fitz seemed speechless when he started his homilies; the readings for those weeks always seemed irrelevant. On the church calendar, we were in that period of "Ordinary Time" between Advent and Lent, just the boring stuff between birth and death.

Still, sermons inevitably turned to Kevin. Lessons were dissected from his corpse in the way a biology class might pillage a dead cat all semester. Kevin, we were told, was enjoying eternal life, both with God and through our stories of him. And on the Last Day, he would return. Many patted me on the back and told me, "You'll see Kevin again."

Kevin's family vanished from the church quickly, and the effect was freeing to the other churchgoers. Stories began to be told. You could almost hear the congregation wishing that Kevin had been a musician as well, as if to confirm their faith and the approval of Saint Cecilia. Maybe in the years to come the neighborhood will say he was and hand his ghost a guitar, once the real story gets blurry and the details become more important. What else can happen when adults act like children, and children like saints?

Darkflips

CLIP WAS A MANIAC on his skateboard that day. He was sticking everything with speed and anger. Roger and I were still trying to land a plain old darkflip on flat ground, but Clip was doing them fakie, off the three church steps, over the banister, even real big off the launch ramp that we had wheeled up to the parking lot. He was an animal, landing everything with teeth gritted. He snarled.

With skating, some kids just get it. Some kids are fearless. We had all seen the trick in a magazine earlier that afternoon, and Clip was already making it his. Other tricks—kickflips, heelflips—had instructive names. They described what they were, how to do it. Kick. Use your heel. But the darkflip—the name itself was on the level of metaphor. It was black—close, in my mind, to something erotic. Even watching Clip stick it, I had no idea what the board was doing.

Clip tried a darkflip noseslide down the banister—pretty nuts—but caught his foot on the railing. He fell, and his skateboard rolled down the long driveway into traffic on Rhawn

Street. Then a Ford Taurus ran it over and split the deck in two. The car didn't even slow down.

At the same time, a guido carrying a basketball was crossing Rhawn Street and saw it all. He laughed at Clip and his broken board, called us "loser fucking skate rats." Clip was on the verge of tears—it was tough to come up with the money for a new deck—but something dark dropped across his face when he heard this.

We hated guidos, and they hated us. And we *were* being risky, skating where we were. The basketball courts—guido territory, for sure—were just across the street from the church, but the church parking lot had just been repaved and the priests never kicked us out. It was a good skate spot.

Clip got up, looked at his skinned hands real fast, grabbed Roger's board, and went straight for the guido. He hit him once across the face with the deck, grip-tape side first, and then once more as the guido fell, again on the head.

There was no traffic on Rhawn Street right then. We were the only people on the planet. The same bad luck that ran over Clip's board, the chaos of the commute, turned good for a minute. We circled the guido. His blood ran around our sneakers.

I expected the priests to come out at any minute—the whole neighborhood even—because the noise that the blow had made was so loud and so like nothing I'd ever heard: a kid getting smashed in the head with a skateboard.

Clip panted. The guido's body sort of hummed on the ground, but I couldn't tell if he was alive or dead. He was a bell that had been rung.

"That was something. . ." Roger said. I thought he was going to finish his thought, but he didn't say anything else.

The world started working again. A light changed somewhere. Another car buzzed past on Rhawn Street. A priest walked out of the church and started toward the rectory. He looked back at us and then looked again.

"Everything okay?"

Roger spoke up again.

"Yeah, Father. He fell. He's just shaken up. Knocked his head."

We were standing in front of the guido like a wall. His blood was running down the driveway onto the street behind us.

"You guys are gonna kill yourselves on those things," the priest said. "You should be wearing helmets."

We all nodded and shrugged, and the priest walked on.

"Let's get him in there," Roger said.

We put the launch ramp up on my and Roger's boards. Then we heaved the guido into the launch ramp so he lay under the plywood on top. He hung on the two-by-fours underneath. Then we wheeled it out of there.

Roger's idea made some sense. Out in the parking lot, anyone could see us; it was a miracle no one had. We needed "time to think," as Roger put it. We were "not trying to kill the kid."

He looked at Clip. "Well, maybe *you* were." Then Roger laughed. It was not a cool laugh.

"My board is still in the street," Clip said. "My trucks and wheels are still good, I think."

"I'll get them," I said, and turned to run toward Rhawn Street. At my back, I heard Roger yell, "Don't think of bailing on us, or we'll tell them you did it!"

Cars bombed by in both directions now. Rush hour. Five o'clock Mass was about to start, and the organ was pumping away inside the church. The two halves of Clip's board were separated by thirty feet in the street. The trucks on both ends were smashed, obviously run over. I waited for the traffic to clear, but it never did. The halves were knocked back and forth across the street, getting more and more useless. I kept watching.

Then a little Honda Civic got one of the trucks caught underneath it. Sparks. The driver slammed on the brakes, was rear-ended. A crowd gathered. Then a cop. I ran off.

We didn't know when the war between guidos and skaters started. Before I ever picked up a board, for sure, for sure. Someone's older brother must have done something to someone else's. It was intraneighborhood, low-level gang shit. But we had the impression this fight went on in every neighborhood, independent of one another. Like something natural.

Guidos were a version of jocks, but it was more complicated than that. They wore cheap gold chains. They played basketball, strictly, but without much seriousness. They were interested in girls more than we were. Typically, they moved in bigger packs than skaters, and an interesting thing about their behavior was that they occasionally fought guidos from other neighborhoods. Skaters would never do that.

Some guidos even used to *be* skaters, but we didn't talk about that.

Clip had been jumped a few months ago by a pack of guidos. He got caught by himself one night, skating home from my house. His board was thrown in some shrubs. He had a black eye for a couple of days. Maybe that's why he did it. Maybe he was mad his folks were splitting up and his mom was moving to New Jersey. Maybe he was upset about something I didn't even know about. The deed being done, how could it matter why?

I had been chased and heckled plenty of times, but I made sure to not get too close to guido hangouts and not travel alone too much with my skateboard. Roger and Clip some-

times called me a pussy about that kind of stuff, but I didn't see
the point in risking it. I stayed unbeaten-up. I ground the hell
out of the curb in front of my own house.

I found Clip and Roger a block and a half away. It was slow
moving with the guido inside the ramp. They were laughing
when I got there.

"Your board's trashed," I reported. "Your trucks just fucked
up some car. A cop was there."

Clip looked seriously hurt. The hundred bucks it cost to get
a new board was never easy for us to come up with. It was
mainly Christmas or birthday territory.

"So. Is it one of them?" I asked. "From before?"

"I'm not sure," Clip said.

"Might as well be," Roger said, and kicked the side of the
ramp as it rolled. "Looks the same to me." He laughed and
knocked on the ramp again. "Who are you, dude? Say something. Identify?"

"Where are we going?" I asked. I pictured a secluded spot in
the woods, some sort of lake we could dump the ramp into.

"My place," Roger said. But that was where we always kept
the ramp.

Clip looked at me. "I want to make sure I got these darkflips
nailed before I lose it."

We pushed and pushed—past smiling neighbors washing
their cars, stickball games, BMXers begging for a shot at the
ramp.

"Nah," Roger told them. "It's cracked. We're taking it back
to patch it up. Later, maybe."

The BMXers shrugged. They spun their handlebars and
wheelied off.

Glops of blood dropped out of the ramp. I heard a moan

no one else admitted to hearing. We were a bad ambulance for sure, for sure.

This was the biggest launch ramp we had ever built. We did this for two reasons. One, for our own egos—bigger, better, etc. Two, to keep the betties and eleven-year-olds away. With a smaller ramp, you get a bunch of tagalongs and jokers who think they can skate it. Every time you push toward the ramp, some little kid snakes you and rides up and rolls back or pussies out in front of you. But this ramp was four feet high. Even we had our reservations about whether or not it was going to be skateable.

It was. You just needed lots of speed, some balls. The betties and eleven-year-olds were scared and kept their distance.

We had not thought of this new reason for the ramp to be so big. We didn't know we were building a coffin at the time. But we had, a pretty good one, too.

The street in Roger's cul-de-sac was a rough and cracked macadam. It could snag wheels and send you flying. Rolling on it, the sound was like thunder. It was not the best place to skate, but it would do. There was no traffic.

At Roger's, we heaved the ramp off of the skateboards, careful to keep the guido inside. No one was watching us.

I was amazed that we had stuffed him in there. He was not a small guido. Inside, he was folded up like some sort of backyard chair. I saw a knee and a bloody ear. I saw a foot on top of a hand. The guido was in a knot under there.

Roger slid Clip his skateboard.

"Do one," he said.

Clip nodded and skated back twenty yards. Then he pushed and pushed at the ramp, and set his feet at the last second.

There was the familiar rumble over the street, the rising note of the wheels on the wood of the ramp, and then the crack at the top as Clip snapped and kicked at the board to get it flipping.

"I'm gonna eat dinner," Roger said. "Help me drag this out of the street."

This time, we didn't put the ramp up on our skateboards. Instead, we just dragged it to the curb, the wood grinding across the cement, the sound of something else scraping underneath. A strange stain was left in the street where the ramp had been, like an oil spot.

"We're just gonna leave it?" I asked. "Overnight?"

"You want me to put a blanket over it? Will that make you feel better?"

Clip was looking up the street, toward home.

"What's the plan here?" I said.

"Why does there have to be a plan?" Roger said. "Why am I, Plan Guy?"

Finally Clip spoke up. "Let's just go," he said.

"Just go," Roger said and then walked in his front door. "Hey, Mom," we heard him say while Clip and I still stood at the curb.

When we get back to Roger's tomorrow, I told myself, the guido will be gone. I was certain of it. He'll come to in the middle of the night, head aching, memory gone. He'll crawl out of the ramp, guessing a little at what had happened. He'll run his tongue around his mouth, maybe spit out a few more teeth. He'll stumble home. His parents will take him to the hospital. The police will come while he lies in bed. He won't be able to give them many details.

We'll take the ramp apart. The priest will think the blood

outside the church was from one of us. The rain will wash it away. The teeth will be crushed under car tires just like Clip's skateboard.

But in the strange moments just before I fell asleep and just after I woke up, there was another feeling. The thrill.

When I got back to Roger's house the next day, Clip and Roger were skating the ramp. I felt relieved.

"Is he gone?" I asked.

"Who?" Clip said.

Roger did a big 180 darkflip off the ramp and caught it backside. Landed it tight, straight, fakie.

"See that?" he said.

Two days ago, that trick was unthinkable to any of us. Yesterday, Roger could barely land its most basic cousin. Now he was flaunting—six feet in the air, board spinning underneath him in a mysterious way, then glued back to his feet. He turned his back to the world, and the wheels kept rolling.

"He's good luck," Roger said and patted the ramp as he skated back.

I wouldn't believe the guido was still in there. They had dragged the ramp out into the street. There were no marks, no sludge, no oil.

I looked inside.

The back of the ramp was like a gaping mouth. We had never nailed a piece of plywood to it, so you could see inside to all the framework. Latticed two-by-fours overlaid with plywood made a big wooden stomach.

Three betties—Julie, Julie, and Michelle—came around with their boards, and Clip and Roger started showing off: 360 kickflips, nollie hardflips, big one-footers. Then the darkflips. The girls sat on the curb, giggled and clapped.

Something was going on, though. Roger and Clip would

not fall. No matter what trick they tried off the ramp, they stuck it. Neither of them had ever been that good.

Roger rolled in front of the girls.

"Wanna see something?" he said.

They nodded.

He walked to the back of the ramp and said, "C'mere."

The betties carried their skateboards like purses. Stickers were neatly organized underneath the deck and matched the wheels. Most of them had pink wheels.

No skate betty lasted much longer than a month or so, maybe a whole summer. They would give up skating for one of a few simple reasons. A bad fall could usually do it. That was the quickest way, but not the most common since they barely rode their boards. Boredom was also an important factor. Watching us try the same tricks over and over again lost its appeal pretty fast. But the most powerful way that they were driven off was ridicule, either from other girls or from us.

"What is it?" one of the Julies asked. All three girls approached the ramp with their arms folded. They didn't trust Roger.

"Just look," Roger said. "We caught something."

A Julie walked to the back of the ramp and looked at the other two girls. Clip was watching vaguely from far off, just rolling his board, an old one he had reluctantly pulled out of his garage, back and forth under his foot. Roger was smiling.

Julie leaned down to look inside.

"What am I looking for?" she asked, then said, "Wait—"

Then she screamed.

I skated toward the ramp. I thought I would hit Roger with my board. Maybe this is how Clip had felt. There was nothing but fear and anger.

Then the Julie laughed, and I stopped. She punched Roger on the arm.

"Asshole," she said.

Roger had snapped her bra strap when she bent down. She didn't see anything. The other Julie and Michelle laughed, too. A small smile even bent Clip's face a little.

"Just skate the ramp, betties," Roger said. "It's magic now."

"It's too big," Michelle said.

"Skate it or leave."

"Fine," one of the Julies said. "I can do it."

"Cool," Roger said and winked at me.

She nailed it. Over and over. Nothing crazy—she was just launching the ramp, no tricks—but no betty had ever skated our ramp before. The other Julie and Michelle were amazed. The first Julie was beaming. Her hair was wild from flying around.

"Told you," Roger said.

The betties skated the ramp all day. None of them fell. Clip and Roger talked them into some spins and grabs. The betties left tired. They had never skated so much. I spent the whole afternoon watching the back of the ramp, half hoping the guido would fall out and end this, whatever was going on. He never did. I hadn't touched the ramp, and Roger called me on it.

"You gonna skate or what?"

"There's a dead kid in the ramp," I said.

"Prove it," Roger said.

I pointed at Clip. "He hit him in the head with his board. Then we stuffed him in there. Yesterday."

"He's a ghost," Roger said. "It's a ghost that's in there."

"We're going to go to jail."

Roger pulled his shirt over his head and yelled, "Boo!"

"Why are we doing this?"

"We skate better."

"Just try it," Clip said.

"Julie saw," I said.

"Try it," Clip said again.

"Julie saw my ass," Roger said. "Julie saw shit."

"Try it."

Roger and Clip—my friends—crowded me, holding their boards. The anger and fear again. But the curve of the ramp was so supple. It was a clear path up that called for wheels.

I backed up and pushed toward the ramp. I pushed as hard as I could, hoping to knock everything loose. I thought of running through the ramp completely, of never leaving the ground but instead smashing the whole thing to sticks, bulldozing it. But two seconds before I hit the ramp, the old instinct kicked in. I set my feet.

And at the top of that ramp, when I snapped and kicked at that board, I felt something—something different—for sure, for sure.

The board spun and turned under me like a whole world. I was above it and in control. Out there in space, even in the middle of the afternoon, it was dark.

When I landed and skated back, Clip said, "Now you get it."

I did.

"There's nothing inside the ramp, is there?" I said.

"Just the inside of it," Roger said.

I was panting. A car pulled into the cul-de-sac and had to drive around our ramp. A guido was picking up a girl. We stared him down.

"There was an earthquake yesterday in California," Clip said. "It looked fun to skate there. Everything was fucked up."

Roger said, "I wanna skate on a nuclear bomb. Grind it."

I said, "I want to be tiny and skate Julie's body."

We were after something. We were compelled to do tricks, like dogs. We threw ourselves at things and destroyed them at the same time. We scraped paint off of railings, scratched marble, and smashed wood. We bought boards and cracked them in half. We launched ourselves into the air with no logical place to land. We fell on our heads. We got back up. We did it again.

A good skater didn't worry. A good skater ignored things like property and pain. It was all in the trick. It was all in the snap and the crack, the sex of gravity, the-spin-the-flip-the-confusion, and then the feel of wheels under you again, solid ground, the howl of polyurethane on macadam. What rules could you break? What could you get away with?

I was 99 percent sure we didn't kill that kid. He probably crawled out of that ramp while I went to look for Clip's board. Or in the middle of the night, like I had hoped. Or maybe we never put him in there at all. It didn't matter. It wasn't death we were after but the trick of it.

This Is Pennypack

THE AUGUST BEFORE NINTH grade, Clip and I found two Indians locked in a cage. We had wandered off the path in Pennypack Park that day, bored. Fishing was useless in the creek by June, and by July, we couldn't even heckle joggers or throw rocks at their dogs. It was too hot. August was always the worst month in Philadelphia. The sky was white with heat; the sun smeared in the humidity and smog. By then, our skateboards were cracked, and the sewers were filled with our tennis balls. Clip and I were tired of each other, too.

At this point in the summer, we hung out with each other out of obligation, out of habit. We didn't talk much. Two weeks before, we had found a wallet while we were off the path. It was pretty much empty, but we looked at the pictures and tried a few infomercials with the one credit card that was left. It was expired. I guess we thought this sort of scavenging might be the last thing left for us to do this summer, picking up the pieces.

The farther we walked from the path, the stranger the things we found. A wallet was not strange. Maybe it was bait.

Clip found a box full of cheap wooden chopsticks, hundreds of them. I found a small garden of Venus flytraps that someone had planted and then abandoned—one even opened its mouth at me. Clip found a framed picture of ballerinas; at the bottom it said, "Degas." He smashed it against a tree. We even found a lizard whose skin was clear, and all its organs just jumping around inside it. It was like I was dreaming, and maybe around the next tree or in the next clearing, whatever I thought of might simply be conjured up.

But the cage we found was black metal, ten feet high, and the size of a small bathroom. Empty bags of potato chips and smashed liquor bottles surrounded the cage. The grass around its edges was dead. The two men inside were shirtless and sunburned. They snored. *I* didn't conjure this up. Clip threw a rock that clanged against the bars, and the two men got up, growling.

The men gripped the cage and glared at us. We stared back.

"What're your names?" Clip said finally. I wasn't going to say anything.

One man said, "No keys."

The other said, "Gotta smoke?"

"Whoa! They're Indians," Clip said. "That's, like, their teepee!"

The wind changed, and we got a whiff of their stink—armpits and waste. No Keys started picking through the empty potato chip bags, looking for crumbs. He ignored us. But Gotta Smoke said his name again, louder this time.

Clip laughed.

"He keeps saying his name like a parrot," he said. "Pretty bird, pretty bird."

"I think he wants a cigarette," I said, and then turned to the Indian. "We don't smoke. We're too young."

"*He* wants firewater," Clip said. "That makes them go crazy. Firewater's booze."

Gotta Smoke sat back down and shut his eyes again. No Keys pissed through the bars in our direction.

"Yes!" Clip said. "Best summer ever!"

Clip had been waiting to say that phrase for months. Wanted specifically to say it after losing his virginity to some homeless beach punk named Sunny, whom he'd dreamed up all spring. He had a whole history for her. During a family vacation, she'd be abandoned by her manic-depressive mother and manipulative stepdad. She'd live under the boardwalk, eating the food and collecting the change that fell through the cracks. Then, one night in Ocean City, New Jersey, Clip would walk past the photo booth in Jilly's Arcade, and she'd drag him in and kiss him, just when the last picture was being taken.

Love would follow. Make-out sessions on the Tilt-A-Whirl. The mad freeing of caged hermit crabs. Second base going down the waterslide. So much graffiti. And finally sex, either on a boogie board that coasted infinitely across the shore, or in the back seat of a fast car driven by one of her older friends, heading back to Philadelphia. Clip hadn't decided yet. He'd have it both ways if he could.

He'd tell this story each night as we sat on the curb in front of my house that summer. It was a bit like a good night prayer, a ritual he needed to perform before sleep. Each night it was a little different, but the fundamental plot points remained the same. Her sun-bleached hair. Her useless family. The impetuous kiss. And when, finally, the Clip in the story got laid, he'd say good night and walk home in the dark heat.

I wasn't sure how I figured into Clip's fantasy. It was *my* parents who rented a house in Ocean City every summer. Clip's dad drove a Greyhound bus. He had wrecked one a few winters back, and was still paying for it. His mom was gone. Clip's family vacation was with us. So I asked him once where I fit in.

"Guess you're stuck with her fat friend, boss," Clip had said.

"Why can't she have another *cute* friend?" I asked. "A girl with black hair. She can hate the beach. We'll stay out of your way."

"She'd like me, too," Clip said.

We watched the Indians in silence for another ten minutes. Clip smiled real big with his mouth open and barely blinked. The men fell asleep again. It was the only thing that made sense for them to do in the heat. Finally, Clip started whispering to me.

"We should go steal some booze and see what they do. My dad has booze."

All I could think about was who put them in that cage. *I* didn't want to get put in a cage.

"We should go," I said.

"You're right," Clip said. "Let's get some supplies." He turned to go and then stopped. "I wish we could leave them a note, but they probably can't read."

It hit me right then that these two men were not Indians. That they were probably just regular old homeless guys, filthy and rough from living in the park. Pennypack was supposed to be filled with them, but they didn't come out much during the day.

I didn't say anything to Clip about that yet. He might have hit me if I did.

Clip was fun to hang out with because he had this poisoned sort of imagination. He was an only child, and was left alone for long periods of time. He was resourceful. And when his dad *was* around, he filled Clip with strange stories from the bus rides. The bizarre stations between Providence and Richmond. The desperate and insane riders. The man whose luggage was a can of house paint. The Mennonites on the way to the beach with a picnic basket. Siamese twins, each holding a replica of the Statue of Liberty. These were the fairy tales Clip grew up on, and the people and places that filled his dreams at night.

And not only was Clip familiar with a cross section of life the rest of us weren't, he had a knack for attracting it. He was the kid who found discarded boxes of porno magazines at the curb on trash night, or who stumbled on two of our teachers making out in a car during recess. If you went to a movie with Clip, the theater would catch fire and you'd get free passes. His dad had passed on a unique way of looking at the world, and Clip wielded it like a magnet.

So it was no surprise Clip found that cage. And if Clip said they were Indians, they were Indians.

On the walk back to the path, Clip made marks on the trees with a knife his dad had given him. His only Christmas present last year, but Clip found a use for it every day.

"We can't forget where they are," Clip said. "They're too cool."

I didn't want to go back. The approaching school year had already started beating the sun down earlier and earlier, and night came fast by eight o'clock. The park was not well lit. And in three days, my family was going down the shore one last time. I wanted to live to see it.

"Dad'll be asleep soon," Clip said. "He's driving at five tomorrow morning. We'll steal some rum to bring back."

"I have to go home soon," I said, and then winced a little bit.

Clip stared at me. I knew he was shocked that I didn't share his enthusiasm. But I'd seen that look before.

"Okay," he said, finally. "At least come back to my house for a minute. We'll plan our attack for tomorrow."

I felt better once we got back onto the path. There were

still some people wandering the park. Joggers. Kids our age. Women with baby carriages. Clip talked out his plan.

"That's how the pilgrims made friends with the Indians," Clip said. "Booze. That's how we took this whole city from them. It's their *weakness*."

We left the park and walked through our neighborhood toward Clip's house. Some kids were still playing stickball in the fading light. Some were doing wheelies on their BMX bikes. I wished briefly that this was still the way we entertained ourselves, too, but that was over. Clip was always stalking new territory.

"Some cigarettes would be good," Clip said. "But those will be tougher to get."

"Food might be easiest," I said, trying to sound helpful. "They look hungry."

"Yeah," Clip said, "but someone is feeding them. Probably whoever put them in there."

Hearing Clip admit that he was thinking of their jailer, too, was somewhat comforting, but he didn't seem threatened.

"Who do you think did that?" I asked. I knew I wouldn't like his answer, but I knew that he also might be right.

"Somebody pretty sick, I bet," Clip said.

Clip's house was in the same development as mine, and was laid out exactly the same inside. But since Clip's mom left, the house had emptied out. Only the bare essentials remained. The living room had a huge TV that sat right on the floor. The cushions on the couch were beat-up rags. Nothing hung on the walls anymore. One pot and one pan, always in the sink. A fridge full of soda and lunch meat and beer. Clip had even attached a small plastic basketball hoop above the doorway in the dining room. The table and chairs were gone now. If we took off our shoes, we were allowed to play there.

Clip's dad was not asleep. He was sitting at the kitchen table, drinking a can of Genesee Cream Ale and reading the *Inquirer.*

"What!" he said as soon as we walked in the door. It wasn't a question.

"Nothing," Clip said. "We found two Indians in Pennypack. They're locked in a cage."

Clip's dad was the only person who scared Clip. And so Clip's dad scared me doubly so. But still, I wasn't expecting Clip to just tell him. I thought it was a secret. The things I didn't tell my parents could fill books.

"Lenni-Lenapes?" Clip's dad asked, not looking up from his paper. "Are they three hundred years old?"

"They stink like it," Clip said. He opened the fridge, took out two sodas, and gave me one.

"Those mopes are always on my Atlantic City runs," Clip's dad said. "They try and scare you by not talking. Totem pole bullshit."

"That's what these two did!" Clip said. "They didn't say nothing. Just their names."

"I'm not impressed," Clip's dad said. "One tried to tell me he was 'Chief of Many Nations' when I was throwing his ass off the bus. I left him at the Camden station." He chuckled to himself. "Indians need tickets, too. *Native Americans.*"

"We're gonna go back tomorrow and mess with them," Clip said. "Maybe they'll sell us some land for our sneakers or something."

"They already have sneakers," I said. "Reeboks."

"Ha," Clip's dad said and looked at me. Then he got up, threw his beer can in the trash, and kissed Clip on the forehead.

"I'm asleep on my feet, boss," he said. "Gotta ride that dog early tomorrow morning." Then he walked out of the room.

It occurred to me then that Clip's dad probably didn't believe a word his son ever said. Why should he? I wouldn't believe him either except I was always right there next to him, staring at whatever Clip had found.

Five minutes after his dad went upstairs, Clip went for the liquor cabinet. He pulled out a bottle of gin. It was unopened.

"This was way in the back," Clip said. "Dad must not drink it."

He cracked the cap and took a swig.

"Yuck," Clip said. "It tastes like a tree. Like a metal tree. They'll love it."

He passed the bottle to me.

"Your dad kisses you," I said.

Clip wiped at his forehead. "No," he said. "Drink up."

I took a small swig. It was awful. I thought that if the Indians drank enough of it, they would die. I coughed.

"Perfect," I said.

I was late meeting Clip the next morning. When I woke up, I peeked out the front window and saw him already across the street, sitting on the curb, carving something into the street with a rock.

I hadn't slept well the night before. In my dreams, Clip and I were always different. He asked *me* questions. He asked me for advice. And I knew the answers. That night, he asked, "Why are those men in cages?" and I said, "You put them there." He asked, "Why would I do that?" and I said, "To punish me." Then he asked, "You did something wrong?" and I wanted to say no to him so bad that I couldn't possibly, the same way as when you open your mouth in a dream to scream and nothing comes out.

"Let's go," Clip said as soon as I came out the door. He wasn't mad, but who knows how long he had waited. "I wanna watch them *feed*."

It was about nine in the morning, and the sun was already

blazing and sending the message that it would be summer forever. It wouldn't. Clip had scratched a big cage into the street with that rock. He'd drawn bar after bar, waiting for me, I guess. The square cage he had drawn was almost completely filled in.

We headed toward the park.

"Got the stuff," he said, and patted his backpack. I heard the bottle of gin rattle against whatever else he brought.

"You still coming down the shore with us?" I asked. It was all Clip had talked about before he found the Indians. "We're leaving the day after tomorrow."

"Huh?" Clip said. "Yeah, yeah." But he was barely paying attention.

We came to the spot on the path that Clip had marked, and he unpacked his bag. The gin was there, wrapped in a T-shirt. Two tuna fish sandwiches. A deck of cards. Three M-8os and a lighter. A copy of *The Last of the Mohicans.*

"What's with the book?" I asked.

"I thought they'd like to read about someone like themselves," Clip said. "I'm supposed to read it over the summer. But it's like five million pages. It's got to go."

The cover of the book showed a shirtless man running and holding a hatchet above his head. He was yelling. He was going to kill someone. Clip was going to a different high school than I was in the fall. He had homework, apparently.

"And the fireworks?" I said.

"Aha," Clip said. "Two things. Our own protection in case things get out of hand. And to trade. Bullets would be better, but they don't have guns anyway."

"What do you want from them?" I said. "Their pants?"

"Not sure yet," Clip said. "Information, maybe."

We trudged through the woods, following Clip's markings. Soon we came to the clearing where the cage stood. The men were huddled in the only corner shaded by the trees. Gotta Smoke nudged the other as we approached.

"We come in peace," Clip said. He held out the sandwiches and the bottle of gin. "Sandwiches. Gin."

The men stood up. They seemed bigger today, much more like the man on the cover of the book. They smiled. No Keys said, "Bring it here."

Clip handed me an M-80 and the lighter and gave me a serious look. Then he approached the cage very slowly as if he were about to pet a wild animal, his hands out in front of him, no sudden movements. The men rocked back and forth on their feet. They *were* wearing Reeboks. Gotta Smoke was wearing sunglasses now, too.

"Let's do business," Clip said. "We want to trade." All the while, he was getting closer to the cage. "What can you bring to the table?"

No Keys snatched Clip's arm and pulled him into the bars of the cage with a clang. Clip dropped the sandwiches, and Gotta Smoke picked them up. Clip was pinned at the shoulder and staring back at me, saying, "Get the gin! Get the gin!" He was holding it out with his other arm as the men were trying to grab it through the bars.

I took it from him, and then backed off. They let Clip go, and he fell back into the grass. Their eyes were on me now, on the bottle.

"No fair," Clip said. He stood up and took the gin and the M-80 from me. He opened the bottle and drank a little. "Mmm," he said. "That's delicious gin. Guess you don't want to trade. Yum."

"We've got to go," I said. I looked around the clearing frantically, expecting their captor any minute. No one came. Just birds. A squirrel.

"You guys are in big trouble," Gotta Smoke said.

No Keys nodded as he ate his sandwich. "Give us the bottle," he said in between bites. "Give it here."

Clip flicked the lighter near the fuse of the M-80. "Tell me something to make me not throw this at you."

"Stay in school," No Keys said.

"Just say no," Gotta Smoke said. They both laughed.

"This could blow your face off," Clip said. "I should blow your faces off for what you did. We're trying to help."

I tugged on Clip's arm. I had noticed something. The door to the cage wasn't locked. When the wind blew hard enough, it rattled and opened a tiny bit before swinging back into place. The situation was weirder than we had thought.

But Clip shrugged me off. He hadn't seen it.

"Fine," No Keys said. "Next time bring roast beef."

"Ham and cheese for me," Gotta Smoke said.

"Next time?" Clip said. "Fine. Tomorrow you guys fess up for sandwiches. And I won't blow you up."

The Indians shrugged and settled back into the shade in the cage. No Keys burped and yawned. We backed out of the clearing and made our way to the path.

On the walk home, I told Clip what I had seen. I tried to explain that they weren't trapped after all. Clip didn't like this. I had taken his Indians and turned them into plain old weirdos. He was angry.

"Why would two people put themselves in a cage?" He said. "What's the point?"

"What's the point of us wandering through Pennypack all the time?" I said. "There's nothing to do."

"Fine," Clip said. "Don't go back tomorrow if there's no point."

"They could kill us," I said.

"You suck," Clip said.

The next morning when I looked out the window, Clip was not waiting for me on the curb. I hung around, expecting a knock on the door. I had been preparing a speech about why I didn't want to mess with the Indians anymore, but he never came. After lunch, I knocked on his door, but there was no answer. I went back home. The house was empty. I thought a lot about the Indians. Maybe they were just two friends like Clip and me, bored. They had found something weird and gone with it.

I watched out the window all day, waiting for Clip to appear. I went to his house again, and his dad finally answered the door. I had woken him up.

"Hey," he said. "Where's Clip?"

"I don't know," I said. "I was coming to find him."

He put his hand on my back and pushed me into the house. I sat on the couch in the living room, and Clip's dad stood between the TV and me.

"So what's going on with the 'Indians'?" he said. "What's he invented now?"

I told him he hadn't invented them. I told him they were real. Just not real Indians.

"Why would there be an animal cage with two human beings *inside* it in the middle of the park?" he said. It was a fair question. I was kind of hoping he had an answer. I didn't offer one.

"What exactly do you guys do in that park? Drink? Do drugs?" He ran both hands down his face like he was exhausted. "I don't get it."

"No, sir," I said. Clip's dad was the only person I called "sir." He made me nervous, mainly because I'd seen him make my own father nervous. Once, at a Fourth of July barbeque, Dad had actually called him "sir," too.

"I know you don't," he said. "But it would make more sense. I mean, when I was your age, I chased girls. And you guys find Indians. I don't get it."

"We'd like to chase girls," I said and thought of Clip's fantasy. Clip wanted to more than I did. "But girls don't really hang out in the park, I guess."

"That's exactly it," Clip's dad said. "What's the obsession with the park?"

Up until that moment, it hadn't occurred to me. Obsessed with Pennypack Park. How could we not be? But I just shrugged. Clip's dad was pacing now.

"Fine," he said. "You're not going to talk. I respect that, boss." He sighed deeply as if he'd just made a tough decision and sat down next to me on the ratty couch. "I'm not around all the time, and I rely on you to look out for him. I do. Maybe I shouldn't say this, but I know you're a good kid. I'm glad you're such good friends. You take him to the beach. You keep him out of the bad stuff he normally wants to get involved in. And I appreciate that."

I thought he'd say more, but instead he looked to me to respond. I was a little shocked by what he'd said. I always thought Clip took care of me. I knew that to be true.

Clip's dad stood up, and I stood up, and he shook my hand.

"I'll tell Clip you were by," he said. "Good night, boss."

By the next night, I still hadn't heard from Clip. We were leaving for Ocean City the next morning. My parents were busy packing, the old joke of my father forgetting to pack underwear getting told over and over again. My sister, Lovely, was wearing her headphones and gave me the finger every time I went into her room to ask for advice. I called Warren to see if he wanted to come down the shore. I didn't tell him about Clip. Or the Indians. He said he had an orthodontist's appointment but could reschedule. I told my parents that Warren was coming instead.

"Where's Clip?" Mom asked. "You guys have a fight? He comes every year."

"He's busy," I said.

"Ha. You guys are getting old," Dad said. "Busy, important future ninth graders. Glad *you* were able to get time off for this though." He pulled a pair of underwear out of his suitcase, stretched and snapped them in my face. "I'm all packed!"

Mom laughed. I went back to my room, put some clothes in a bag, and went to sleep.

Warren and I had a lot of fun in Ocean City. During the day, we went crabbing with Dad in the bay or walked the beach looking for interesting trash. Warren found a washed-up bikini top. I found a warm, unopened beer. Warren found some sort of steering wheel. I found another empty wallet. Last year, they closed this beach because of the stuff people found on it.

At night, we paced the same four blocks of boardwalk for hours. There was nothing we wanted to buy. We considered roller coasters, then saw the line. We were just old enough to be impatient and bored by those things. So we looked for girls, preferably another group of two. We found one. It was really easy. When we asked their names, they told us. Janet and Julie. They were sunburned. They said, meet us at the 12th Street beach tomorrow. We did. They wore bikinis. It was incredible.

When we said good-bye to the girls, Janet looked like she might cry. She took my hand and walked me farther down the beach. She handed me a letter and kissed me. It wasn't sex on a boogie board, but it would do.

We passed Clip's house as we drove home. He was outside, bouncing a tennis ball off of his garage door. My dad honked, and Clip looked and held up his hand to the car.

"Guess his important business meetings are over," Dad said. "Maybe he made some money." Mom laughed, and Warren looked at me, puzzled. I shrugged.

Back at the house, Lovely came into my room while I unpacked. She hadn't gone on the trip. She was always jealous for a half an hour when we came home from things she claimed she didn't want to do.

"What's wrong with your friend?" she said. "He's weird."

"What do you mean?" I said. "Clip?"

"I don't know," she said. "He came by here looking for you. He had paint all over his face. I think he was drunk. Like in the middle of the day." She sat down on my bed, something she normally wouldn't do. "I didn't know you guys drank. He must have been coming from some party."

"What do you mean, 'paint'?" I said.

"I don't know. Like under his eyes. Down his nose." She got up and crossed to the door. "Whatever. So did you geeks meet some hot beach bunnies?"

"Yeah," I said.

After Lovely left, I reread Janet's letter two or three more times. She said, "Come visit." She said, "Your eyes are so pretty." She said, "You only live a train ride away, across the bridge to Lindenwold." She said, "I'll miss you."

After dinner, I grabbed a tennis ball and went for a walk. The sun was below our development then in the gray-and-orange haze. I missed the beach. The clear sky. The biplanes trailing messages. Clip was not outside his house. His dad's car was in the driveway, and I guessed they needed their time together. I didn't knock. We weren't friends for a week, and it broke my heart.

I wrote letters back to Janet. I had never mentioned Clip to her, so I pretended I was him. I tried to be exciting and frightening. I told her:

"I found two Indians in the park. They're wild, but we've become friends. We drank gin and painted our faces. Gin tastes like trees. Metal trees. I watch them feed. I'm not scared of high school because this has been the best summer ever. I miss you."

I stalked the neighborhood for a week, the last one of the summer. No sign of Clip. I even went back to the cage, following Clip's marks, and it was empty and turned on its side. On my walk back to the path, I found a copy of a book called *On the Beach*. The picture on the cover was of a couple holding hands as the sun set over the ocean. I put it in my back pocket, thinking of Janet. I found a calendar with every day but today X-ed out. I left it there. Then I found a tennis ball, neon green in among the brown of the summer-scorched park. I kept that, too.

Then Clip was outside, as if I'd summoned him with my search, hurling his own tennis ball at the front of his house. His dad must have been at work. The ball dented siding and smudged windows and left pockmarks in the garage door. I threw my own ball over his head as a means of saying hello.

"Hey," he said.

We threw the balls for a while until he finally just threw his on the roof.

"How was the shore?" he said. There was no paint on his face. It was plain old Clip.

"It was fine," I said. "You know the drill. Beach. Boardwalk. Beach again." I couldn't tell him about Janet.

He nodded. "Give me that," he said, pointing to my tennis ball. I tossed it to him.

"What's up with the Indians?" I said. He knew this was the real question.

"Fucking idiots," he said. Then he slammed the ball in the small space between the kitchen windows. "They got boring."

"Everything does," I said, but didn't believe that. Janet was not boring. Not yet.

"School starts soon," he said. "It'll be weird going different places."

"It sucks," I said. "I hate my parents, I do." My parents wanted me to go to school out of the city. It occurred to me now that maybe they wanted me away from Clip. But I hadn't complained to them at all.

"You'll be fine," he said. "Honors classes. *Pool* class. It's not even like real school. I'll be going through metal detectors. I can't believe you didn't get homework."

"At least there will be girls there," I said. This prep school my parents had picked out for me was all boys. I produced the book from my pocket. "I did," I said, "get homework."

He looked at the cover of the book and then launched the ball to hit the house like a pop fly. It was mine to grab. I got under it, spun around, and tried to catch it behind my back. It didn't work. Clip laughed and snatched up the ball as it rolled down the street.

"Well, I'm asleep on my feet, boss," he said. "I'll see you tomorrow?"

It was a question now.

"Yeah," I said. "I'll come by."

"You kissed a girl in Ocean City," he said. I thought of his father, of Clip's forehead.

"No," I said. I touched my face. "You put those guys in a cage."

"No," he said. "I let them out."

"I don't ever want to go back to Pennypack again," I said.

Clip said, "Okay. We won't."

Chase Us

CLIP AND I RUN Pennypack Park with a carton of cigarettes, knocking over the joggers. He goes for the ankles from behind. When the joggers fall, he hangs over them and blows a lungful of smoke in their faces. The joggers cringe into little balls, waiting for a second hit that never comes. Then I follow Clip off into the woods.

We keep running.

I light two cigarettes in my mouth and hand him one. We both have the same cold sores from sharing, but in opposite corners of our mouths. Mine has gotten especially bad, and I can't open my mouth all the way. We hope to achieve good health from all the running because the park is hilly. But we've got no air from the smokes. We wheeze.

There's nobody for a while. The early-morning joggers are gone, so we smoke off the path up in the woods like two Indians. The city is above us, surrounding the park, and below it, too, in the subways.

We talk a little.

"I'd like a little music out here. A radio," Clip says. He dances a bit, kicking up leaves. He opens another pack of cigarettes.

"Have you hit the same guy twice yet?" I say. Do they come back to the park, is what I want to know.

"Hard to tell from behind," Clip says.

"But you do look them in the face," I say.

Clip just shrugs. He pinches his smoke between his thumb and pointer. I try to hold it like that but end up biting my fingers.

A mountain biker speeds past on the path, catching us off guard. Clip can only yell a curse, smoke curling around his mouth as he does it.

The moms are out walking their babies. By then my heart rate is way up from twenty-five cigarettes, and the veins in my arms and legs ache. Clip's voice is gone from all our smoking and yelling, but still he's full of great gestures. He pumps his hips at the mothers.

Clip's told me he wants to get into this, and I don't know if I think it is a good idea. His main worry is that he'll be maced.

"They don't bring purses usually," Clip says. "They probably won't have mace with them, right?"

"Some of them have pepper spray key chains," I remind him. "Some stab with car keys."

He lights a new cigarette from the old one.

"I just don't want them burning these baby blues out."

Clip's eyes are gray, definitely gray, and I wonder if he's ever seen himself. He must have, though. There are mirrors in our bathroom where we sleep.

Then Clip jumps on my back, whooping and smacking my behind. I carry him through the trees and the branches cut my arms, but I don't want to stop because I know he doesn't want me to.

∙ ∙ ∙

I just started following Clip around. He called to me once while I was fishing off of Big Rock. I ignored him. I thought he was crazy. He came out to the rock and redirected my pole. I still caught nothing.

"Forget it," he said. "Come watch this."

We hid twenty feet off the path for ten minutes. He didn't say anything. Finally, a Rollerblader came around the bend, and Clip flew onto the path, knocking the guy over, out of his helmet even. When the guy finally got up, he looked around frantically, and hiding and spying on that was like nothing I've ever felt.

When night fell, and Clip made no move to leave the park, I stayed, too. He asked me questions about my life, about Mom and Dad specifically. We sat on the bathroom floor and smoked, and I told him that once, while swimming, Dad had called me a "pirate's dream." I had always liked that. Clip laughed and told me the punch line I never got: a sunken chest. That hurt. I told him sometimes Mom would still rub my back until I fell asleep. This made Clip angry. He pounded his fist on the tile. He said, "It's best that you're here."

Now, I carry the cigarettes and the tackle box, which is full of cash. I also do all the talking when we go back into the neighborhood to buy more smokes and sandwich stuff while Clip paces outside. I don't do much actual hitting in the park. It's not for me.

But I do wonder sometimes what Mom and Dad might think about all of this. Would they really be surprised? Are they looking for me?

Clip had a theory about Pennypack Park. It was "off the map," he said. It was "perched under" the rest of the world. The rules no longer applied.

At first, this made no sense to me. I pointed down the path

and said, "Fox Chase is that way." I turned around, "Lawndale is that way. East. Then the Delaware River."

He shook his head at me. "Northeast Philadelphia is a myth," he said. "Names don't mean anything."

"What does that make us?" I said.

He ignored my question, but as proof of his earlier point, he opened his tackle box. Clip said, "Where does all that money come from?"

"I thought it was yours," I said.

"Where would I get all of that money?" he said. "Does it seem like I have a job?"

I shrugged. I figured he robbed people.

"You think I took that money from people in the park?" he said.

I shrugged again.

"You insult me, little brother," he said. "That money has been *given*. By all of this." He raised his arms to the treetops and spun around slowly.

There's another mom coming down the path, pushing a carriage, walking her baby in the sunshine. Pretty through our smoke.

"If you see a mom pull something out, give a yell," Clip says.

"Probably not a macer," I say. He just nods, prayerful like he gets before he takes off. "What exactly are you going to do?"

Clip breaks from the trees down onto the path, leaving a trail of smoke behind him like a bad car. The mom screams, and he grabs both sides of the carriage and blows a big cloud onto the baby. Then he takes off across the path on the other side, hooting.

The mom finally stops screaming. She picks the baby up and runs back the way she came with the kid at her shoulder, crying. I think she saw me.

When she's gone, I come out of the trees and examine the carriage she left behind. It's a nice one: thick blue plastic, good bearings in the wheels, roomy. I put the carton of cigarettes and the tackle box in it and roll it through the woods, trying to find Clip.

With Clip, no one fights back, though I think many could chase him down, catch him, and beat him in a fight. Actually, we're both skinny and weak, though we hope for strength in the future. But Clip's smoke blowing is mysterious and frightens people. I don't have the confidence yet, and I don't scare anyone. Except now, I'm thinking about what that mom must have thought who saw me up in the trees. Seeing me up there, she thought I was the real threat, and Clip only a diversion. When she turned to run, she expected me on her back with a knife. I just know it, the way that mom looked at me.

I finally find Clip half a mile off the path on the banks of the creek. He's huffing between puffs on his cigarette, his hands on his hips.

Clip says, "Well, what did she do?"

"She took off running," I say.

Clip says, "You brought the carriage. Shit."

"What?" I say.

Clip says, "What are we gonna do with it? It's evidence." He grabs the carriage and starts to roll it into the creek.

"Wait!" I say.

He stops, and I grab the carton out of it. We smoke another cigarette. Minnows circle the wheels of the carriage and take little bites.

"How was it?" I say finally.

Clip says, "Great. It was great."

"Are you gonna do it again?" I say.

Clip says, "I think we should."

"I'm gonna keep the carriage," I say.

Clip says, "For what?"

"Keep stuff in," I say.

Clip says, "I think I hurt my ankle coming down that hill." He takes his shoe off and shakes out a few rocks.

"If the cops come, I'll say I found it," I say. "Because she just left it. I could have found it like anyone else."

Clip says, "You know there's no cops." He wades into the cold creek. "My ankle. It's swelling up."

I wheel the carriage back out of the creek up onto the bank and try to dry the wheels with the baby blanket so they don't rust. I put the carton of cigarettes back in it with the wet blanket and the tackle box. The lunchtime joggers will be coming soon, but Clip doesn't seem interested in getting out of the water. He's talking.

Clip says, "Wonder if the mom will send the dad down here to look for us. That carriage might get you beat up, if so. That's my only point."

"She didn't see me," I say.

Clip says, "Yes, she did. She was watching you up in the trees the whole time. They always watch you."

"You're the one tackling and hooting."

Clip says, "And you're the weirdo watching. They expect worse from you. Me, too."

Then Clip just dunks himself, cigarette and all, into that grimy, cold creek.

Clip's ankle is bad, and he doesn't want to chase anyone else for the rest of the day. It's become big and ugly and wrinkled, like a purple cantaloupe. We smoke out on Big Rock with him dangling his leg into the cold water to help the swelling. Some kids are fishing nearby, and Clip is yelling instructions at them from the rock.

"If you kids had some raw hot dogs, you'd do much better!" Clip says. "Your mom and dad shouldn't have bought you all that nice gear!"

The kids just look at us. One has some sort of black box that he's pointing at the water. The other two cast their complicated poles where he points.

"Why don't you want to chase them out?" I say.

Clip says, "Well, they might be you and me someday. The older people, we already know."

Just then, one of the kids pulls out two nice-size sunfish on one hook, and they all cheer. Pennypack is a strange place.

Clip curses, and when he pulls his ankle out of the water, I see it throb.

"Why not blow smoke in their faces?" I say.

Clip says, "Is that a dare?"

"Just a question," I say.

Clip says, "You want to watch, don't you, you sick maniac?"

He limps across the water, splashing and hopping. All but one of the kids get away, and Clip pins him by his shoulders to the bank. A healthy Clip would have caught all three of them. He would have flown across that water without even getting wet. I've seen him do it.

"Get over here!" he yells at me. "Bring the smokes!" I'm still sitting on Big Rock. The kid is crying, with Clip half burying him in the mud. The fish are trying to bounce back into the water but are still on the hook. His two friends are up in the woods, watching. I see them.

Clip says, "Hold him down a minute for me!" I grab the kid, and Clip sits in the mud, holding his ankle. "My foot is numb! My whole leg!"

The kid spits on me, sensing that I'm not Clip. He saw me hesitate. So I take a huge huff of my cigarette and blow big in the kid's face. His friends run.

We keep the kid until after the park closes, so he is kidnapped. This was my idea. They will come for us now and we want that, I think. We must.

The three of us head back to where we sleep, one of the public bathrooms in the park. We shut the door behind us and run the hot water in all the sinks for as long as it works to heat the place. We sleep under the pipes.

The kid—we name him Roger—has gotten agreeable and falls asleep first. We think he is like us. I know I have moved, somehow, closer to Clip, doing what I did. He is so sweaty he takes his shirt off and coughs in his sleep. But when his chest and stomach tighten up like that, it's a nice sight.

And Roger is a beauty, too. He sleeps through sunrise, and the smell coming off of him is like some kind of fruity cereal. Awake, he doesn't seem surprised at all to see me staring at him. He walks right over and takes a cigarette.

Clip is whispering to Roger while I push the carriage behind them. Every once in a while I hear a little of the conversation.

"The name 'Pennypack' comes from an Indian word meaning 'inside the mind of the bear there is music.' Did you know that?"

Roger blinks. "Which tribe? Lenni-Lenape?"

Clip has never spoken of this with me before.

"An *Indian* tribe, kid! *Our* tribe. What does it matter? And where we're standing right now used to be ten feet under water."

I look up, expecting a wave to crash down onto the path. Instead, I trip on a crack in the macadam. Roger and Clip keep walking and whispering.

· · ·

We get to one of the good straightaways and start running. Roger is fast, but Clip seems slowed by his ankle. The leaves are turning up like it's going to rain. We hear a whirring—looks like two on mountain bikes are coming toward us. We think between me and Clip and Roger and the carriage we can get a good hit.

Roger's in. I'm in. But as the bikers get closer, something seems off. They must see us, but they pick up speed. We pick up speed. We start yelling.

Clip leads with his shoulder but hits the biker dressed in orange like he's a wall and collapses. Roger, getting the idea, gives a jump kick that completely misses and then runs into the trees, laughing. I purposely steer away from the bikers, but my carriage topples over at that speed and the cigarettes and tackle box spill out. The biker dressed in yellow gets off his bike and kicks me in the stomach when I bend over to pick up the smokes. Then I play dead.

Clip tries to run, but his bad ankle gives. The biker in orange hangs over Clip and jabs him in the stomach. The biker in yellow finally pulls the biker in orange off, and they ride on down the path.

Roger comes back, obviously enthused. He pretends to do some more karate, and hoots and bounces around us. Then he sees the blood on Clip's shirt.

"You're dead!" Roger yells happily.

"I'm fine!" Clip says. "But stabbed. I think they knew we were coming." He looks at Roger. "This never happens."

The rain starts full on. We go back to the bathroom, and Clip tries to clean the wound in the sink. He gnashes his teeth when the soap hits.

"I think that guy hit me with his water bottle," he whispers. "The crazy fuck sharpened the plastic top."

His explanation doesn't make much sense, but the wound is messy and ragged. When Clip presses on the sides, it opens like a mouth. I think Clip told Roger that the jogger had hit him with an axe or something. I let it go.

I try to get Clip to go the hospital, but he tells me, "We can't leave the park. You know that."

I'm not sure he's right. We've been out of the park plenty of times. But I know I can't help him. Even if he has stopped bleeding on the outside, he may still be bleeding on the inside.

Three days pass like this. Clip screams at night in his sleep. His wound leaks orange and black and smells like a garbage disposal. His ankle has gotten worse, too. His entire leg is swollen like a rolled-up carpet and too big to use. Roger and I heave him into the baby carriage and ease him down the path in the morning.

Roger says, "Don't you guys eat?"

"If we find a picnic," I lie. I'm afraid if I open the tackle box, it will be empty.

Roger says, "Can we find a picnic?"

"I don't know," I say. "Looks like it might rain again."

"Okay. Watch this!" Roger yells, and spins a big cartwheel down the path and keeps running.

Clip starts talking from the carriage.

"This park is all there is. That kid is a wolf. He wanted to get caught by us. Don't forget it. The mom was scared, mainly of you. Give me a cigarette."

Clip is in a coma, I think, and snoring, too. The park is blue in the mornings when we can't see the sun yet over the trees. We startle some deer while we walk. The mist coming off the creek makes me feel unsettled. It's like the steam out of sewer caps.

"What are we doing out here?" Roger finally asks, practically skipping, and I realize he's talking to me. I'm in charge now. Clip just moans and drools. Roger and I have another cigarette. Now the kid is blowing the smoke out of his nose. He shows his teeth, too, when he does it.

"When I think of myself," I tell the kid, "this isn't it. But I guess it is. I'm sorry."

"It's okay," Roger says. "No school!" He takes off running and I try to keep up, pushing sick, delirious Clip in the baby carriage. The path forks, and to the left is the way out of the park, to Lawndale. Roger is stopped when I get there, staring up toward the exit. The morning fog still hasn't burned off, and the exit to the park is just a bright mist. There are shadows moving in it, but nothing we can make out.

"Should we leave?" I ask either of them, not knowing who is more capable at this point. Roger leans into Clip's wound and holds his nose.

"He stinks."

Just then, Clip starts up, knocking Roger back, and gets out of the carriage. A pink cream drops out of his stomach wound. Roger laughs and pretends to puke, but all I can do is squeeze the handle on the baby carriage tighter.

Clip looks at us like he's never seen us before and limps up the path toward the exit. When he hits the mist, it doesn't look like he's walking anymore. The path disappears and he is just a rising shadow, and that finally disappears, too.

We go the other way.

Dad never comes looking for me. We still use the carriage. Roger's friends never come looking for him. No cops ever. Clip was right.

When I was a kid in this park, I remember, Dad would point into the woods and pretend to see Indians. I would always just miss them. Later, I learned that the park was actually filled with the drugged homeless. But now I get it. I am the Indian no one sees, just hunching and ignored. Watching. Imagine that.

Now, the joggers and moms come and go and we don't bother with them too much. We hide and watch from up in the trees, maybe throw rocks. Roger is getting bigger every day, and bristling and anxious, but I insist for now on just lurking and watching. He listens. He does fake karate against the trees, but he listens to me.

The tackle box is empty. I raise my hands to the treetops and spin around, but nothing happens. We're out of food.

Roger says, "Where's Clip?"

"He'll be back," I say.

He says, "Did Clip take all of the money? I'm hungry."

"He didn't take it," I say. "It was given to him."

So Roger brings butchered squirrels and sparrows back to the bathroom at night and cooks them over his cigarette lighter. I do not know how he catches them. He's not like me and Clip. He won't speak to me about his home when I ask, about his mom and dad. He doesn't wonder if they miss him. I think I'll have to let him loose one of these days, or he might kill me.

But I am not lying when I say Clip will come back. I know this is true. The moms came back. The joggers, too. We will always be friends and I'll always be watching him. He'll appear and call to me again, and I'll follow.

The Kidnapped and the Volunteers

ROGER BUYS A SCHOOL bus, a small one used before by the Korean church gone under. Five hundred bucks at the bank auction got him this, and on its side is painted "Repent Sinners."

That night, Roger bombs around town with all the lights going like an ambulance, the stop sign on the side out like a wing as he flies through the neighborhood. Clip and I stand on the corner, drugged and locked out of our apartment because we both lost our keys.

Roger pulls up and throws open the door to the bus.

"Get in, kiddies!" he says. "You'll be late for school."

I back up, not recognizing him from under a blanket of ether. Clip gets on and looks back at me, his wits still somehow about him. Then a dog barks in the night, and I run onto the bus.

Something extra kicks in, and I'm convinced I have to keep running inside the bus to stay on board. I jog in place and don't hear much of their conversation, just what Roger yells. Ether turns the volume of the world up and down in pulses, like dunking your head in and out of water.

"I'm gonna teach! I have knowledge! And now this bus!"

Well, he does have the bus.

"The wonders of medicine!" he says. "This town is sick!"

Finally, I collapse into a seat a few back from the front. The ether rag is still tucked into the front of my shirt like I'm at a restaurant.

"How about we eat something?" I say.

Roger glares at me over his shoulder and the bus slides into the oncoming lane. "This is serious."

So I just lean against the cool glass of the window and think about how earlier that day I saw Korean Janet eating slices of some kind of magnificent green fruit on the ledge outside the salon, juice on her chin, her eyes closing with each bite.

When they're through talking and Roger finally drops us off, Clip and I try to sleep in the azalea bushes next to our apartment. Lying there, I whisper to Clip, "What did you say the name of that fruit was again?" The memory goes with this stuff, too.

"*Kiwi*. Christ, write it down."

"Kiwi," I mumble. Fantastic.

The Korean church went under because the Korean dry cleaners did. It was taken as a bad sign by the congregation, and many abandoned their new religion.

The Korean dry cleaners went under because lots of places have. Northeast Philadelphia is reeling under white flight and the allure of the suburban mall. The only place left now is the Korean nail salon where the white women still get sharpened and painted. The Korean men avoid the place. Instead, they wander the neighborhood like tolerated pigeons. God and money have left them.

Clip and I fell out of state college like there was a slide attached to it. Classrooms ejected us. Fraternity parties were places where we got beat up, and we never liked the taste of beer. But we did manage to steal as much ether as we could carry from the biology lab.

Roger's from the neighborhood and was also in our biology class—premed—though Clip insists no real doctor ever went to state college. Roger was the guy with his hand up constantly, but never with the right answer. He always did the opposite of the experiment—shocked frogs back to life, spread mean viruses from dish to dish. He stayed in school and abused loans. Clip and I left.

Now we work as "lunch aides" at Saint Cecilia's Elementary, keeping the uniformed kids inside the cones in the parking lot where they have recess. My sister, Lovely, teaches fourth grade and got us the job.

She threatened us, "Mess this one up and you can rot. One kid gets hit by a car, and you're no longer my brother." She pointed to Clip. "That goes double for you."

Lovely's a sad girl who lives for knowing more than ten-year-olds. Now that our parents are dead, the ghost of our mother haunts her frame, and I can tell she wants to ground me.

I'm also in love with Korean Janet. Her cheekbones are as high as heaven, shoulders broad like a swimmer's. She works in the nail salon, but I see her everywhere: taking her dog for a checkup at the animal hospital, putting extra butter on her popcorn at the movies, cutting coupons in the Mayfair Diner on Sunday afternoons. Her eyes are like two hooded thugs.

Janet is serious. A student. A Christian. A kiwi eater.

Roger pulls duct tape across the "Repent Sinners" sign on the side of the bus, but keeps all the crosses intact. We see all these little heads in the windows behind him when the bus speeds past our corner in the morning.

Clip and I still haven't found our keys. We catch up on sleep in the faculty lounge during the day when the teachers are teaching, and then work the lot when it's recess time.

"Ah," Clip says, smiling, eyes closed, and stretched out on the couch. "The good old days."

"Which were those?"

"You know. Eating crayons. Nap time. Sniffing glue. It's good to be back at school."

I realize he's raided the supply closet.

"Gimme," I say. "Share the wealth."

He tosses me a tiny bottle of Wite-Out. I'm overzealous and get paint on my nose.

"Easy," Clip says. "This stuff is nontoxic."

He's right. The headache hits immediately, but still, it's like hammering at a pillow. We gurgle on the couch until ten thirty, and then go out on the lot to set up the cones. The space we mark out is ragged.

First lunch period and the youngest kids pour out of the cafeteria, burping bologna and cheese. They like me and Clip, and show off a little for us. One kid stands on his hands, falls, scrapes his face. Another grabs the girls' skirts and drags them around the lot. One tightens his little Catholic tie until his face turns blue and he faints. We laugh, then blow our whistles, and they stop.

But out there on the lot, something isn't right. Even we can tell, high in the huffing clouds and all. Some kids are missing.

After work, Clip and I go to Pennypack Park, sniff antifreeze under the trees. We're rationing the ether we've got—about a gallon of lab-grade stuff that should keep us floating for a good couple weeks if we're careful. We get dumb, and the feel of the grass is so perfect I take my shoes off.

The Korean men gather there in the afternoons, too, feed the pigeons, twist their mustaches. Some of their wives work in the salon with Janet. Some of their wives have gone back to their old country, I think; there are fewer than there used to be. The men talk to one another in Korean, words that rhyme with "sing" and "pow," and we think they sound angry. One stands up on a picnic table—the ousted preacher—and shouts. His strange eyes are huge behind oversize glasses, his button-up shirt untucked. The other men smoke their tiny cigars and nod.

Clip and I call the old preacher "Duk," and make fun of him. We make the sign of the cross like karate chops at each other, say, "Fatha! Sahn! Horly Shpirit!" Soon we're wrestling full-on and roll out of the woods, laughing. The Koreans get up and leave.

Still can't find our keys. We tried the windows to our apartment with no luck. We don't know the landlord's number and would be afraid to call it if we did. At first we thought, they'll turn up. Then we started to think, maybe we don't need to get inside.

"We could just live in this park," Clip says. "Everything we need is here. Water, food. *Air.*"

I'm not so natural a person, and complain about the phone calls I might miss, hair conditioner, clean underwear.

"We'll wear big leaves as underwear and shave our heads. And here's our new phone." Clip cups his hands around his mouth and shouts, "9-1-1! I'm having a heart attack! The baby is breeching!"

Some sparrows stir and the leaves shake, but no one comes to the rescue.

• • •

Korean Janet has never lost a key, to be sure. She rolls her loose change—tips from the salon, I guess—and takes them to the bank in big linen bags. My room in the apartment I'm locked out of is littered with nickels I'll never count or spend. I'm almost too lazy to be rich.

I asked her once if she needed help carrying her bags of change, but she beat me off like a thief, saying things like "sing!" and "pow!"

But she does have a rump on her. Even Clip will admit this.

He says, "Quite a back seat for a foreign car."

Roger shows up at the Mayfair Diner, complaining and wearing a stethoscope. Clip and I eat stacks of pancakes late at night because there's no time in the morning before work and the ether makes us starving.

"Damn Koreans keep throwing fruit at my bus."

It's out there in the lot, parked sideways across a whole row of spots, a fan in the engine still growling. A table of Korean men looks up from their coffee across the diner. One points.

"Maybe they don't like that you crossed out their message," Clip says. "It's a good one, you know."

"Maybe they're upset their church went under," I say.

"Is this still America?" Roger says, pouring the spilled coffee in his saucer back into the cup. "Yes. Am I God? No. One threw a whole cabbage at me while I was driving. That's dangerous."

"Where did you take those kids you picked up today?" Clip asks very casually, his mouth full of pancake.

Roger stares him down for a second. "Nowhere."

"You better watch yourself. They're looking for a kidnapper."

"It's not kidnapping if they just get on. They can make their own choices. Plus, I have a school."

"Cops might see it different. Moms and dads will, too, I think."

"You guys give advice now? At least I got *keys.*" He dangles them in front of us like we're babies and downs his coffee. "Let me know if you want me to ram your door down with my bus so you two can get some sleep."

Roger leaves and pulls out of the lot, honking. Everyone in the diner grimaces. He's the problem no one knows how to solve yet.

Duk and the Koreans are at our corner the next morning when Clip and I stumble out of the bushes, kicking bottles of windshield-wiper fluid with us, still in a bad huffing haze.

"Where our bus?" Duk asks. The other men nod at one another, like, *Yeah, good question.*

"Don't know, Duk," Clip says. "But we gotta go to work. Can't talk." He has pink flowers and twigs sticking out of his hair.

Duk says, "Duk?"

Clip points at him—"You Duk"—then pokes himself in the chest—"Me Tarzan."

"We see you with him. Where he now? Row-ger."

"I don't know, Duk." Clip bends down to tie his shoe. "In your bus maybe?"

The Koreans circle up and chat, and then follow us all the way to the school, ten feet back and silent, like a pack of dogs waiting for us to croak. But they stop at the door to the school like there's a hex over it.

Inside, Clip snores on the couch, peaceful, but no amount of rubber cement can relax me. Finally, someone needs us to pour sawdust on some second grader's puke. I go do it.

At lunch, when we come out of the teachers' lounge, the Koreans approach the parking lot, yelling, "Where children?"

Duk's right. More kids are missing, some of theirs now. Clip and I stand at opposite corners of the lot with only thirty kids between us, and they're docile and confused by their friends' absences. They hover in the middle, maybe afraid they'll disappear, too.

Clip is annoyed. I can see the huffing headache sitting on his brow. "Don't know the answer to that one either, Duk. Lots of things are missing. For instance, where are our keys?"

Duk seems to know he's being insulted, but is not sure how. He lights a miniature cigar, says, "Something not right."

"You said it, Duk."

Then a kid on Clip's side runs past the cones toward Rhawn Street. I blow my whistle, and the kid freezes. A tennis ball rolls down the long driveway into lunchtime traffic.

"Tell you what, Duk," Clip says. "I'll make you a deal. Find our keys and I'll find your kids."

Lovely grabs us before we go home from work.

"What's going on? Where are the kids? What's with the Koreans?" Lots of questions we can't answer.

She tells us the receptionist spent all afternoon calling parents to ask them why their kid was absent with no excuse. She tells us none of the parents knew their kids weren't going to school; they're always home by three o'clock, safe and sound.

I say, "Roger?" and Lovely punches me in the arm. They had a thing once, and she knows we're sort of like friends.

"You two better not be involved in this." She stamps off toward her car in a cloud of chalk dust.

Clip shouts, "Can we stay with you tonight?"

I've considered getting a manicure for the chance to talk to Korean Janet. I've vowed—Clip as my witness—to learn Korean. I don't do either.

Instead, I just watch her, hoping to become like those nature photographers who eventually seem to the animals to be just another gazelle or plant in the background. I want to be a piece of furniture she walks by, maybe sits on. I watch her on her bike with the basket and bell. To and from the nail salon, looking fresh as she enters and tired when she leaves, still beautiful. Then up the stairs to the El platform wearing a backpack full of schoolbooks.

I go to a grocery store and find what they say is kiwi fruit, but they're just brown and hairy, none of that brilliant, juicy green I saw before. I buy two, intending to confront Clip about it.

That night, I come back to the corner, exhausted from following her. Clip, already lounging in the azalea bushes, passes me a plastic bottle with a rag in it. "Sniff what I got out of the salon dumpster."

I give it a whirl. It's a sour, metallic burn—most taste happens in the nose, so it's a lot like drinking nail polish remover. It's exactly like sniffing it.

"You're not actually falling for the preacher's daughter, are you?" Clip says.

"She's Duk's?" The thought hadn't occurred to me. But I guess Clip is watching her, too, and doing a better job.

"Of course. She looks exactly like him. Saw him kiss her on the head in the salon. You think she's gonna be a hellcat in the sack because she's the minister's daughter or something?"

"I'd just like her to say something to me in English at this point."

"So you just think it's interesting she's from Mars? And hope she thinks vice-versa?" Clip takes a huff and says, holding his breath, "Ain't gonna happen." *Cough!* "This ain't that movie."

"Anyway, it wasn't kiwi. Look." I hold the two hairy bastards out in what I think is a small victory.

"Here. Gimme." Clip rips the top off one, and there it is—neon joy. There's hope after all.

• • •

When we wake up the next morning, I notice Clip's nails are trim and clean. Mine aren't. Roger speeds past, and kids I recognize smile in the windows and wave back, the bus pointing distinctly away from the school.

"Maybe we should follow him," Clip says. But the bus is already out of sight.

On the lot at recess, twenty kids shuffle around. I don't have to blow the whistle once.

A few cops stroll up to talk to Clip and me.

"So where are all the kids?" one says.

Clip has hit the ether at work today—something we swore we would never do—and does all the talking.

"Not at school. You guys call it 'truant,' I think."

"Think something bad is going on here?"

I can see Clip framed in one of the cop's mirrored lenses and me in the other.

"They ain't learning their multiplication tables, if that's what you mean."

"You know what I mean."

"I do. But Officer, these kids here depend on me for their safety. And every question you ask me is a *distraction*. So if you don't mind."

The cop turns to me and says, "Well?"

I say, "I don't have kids. Don't know what they do, but you might want to ask—"

Clip interrupts me.

"While you're here though, I would like to report a robbery. Someone stole our keys."

Saturday is quiet. Clip is gone when I wake up, so I go to Lovely's house. She's drinking pink wine with ice and crying when I get there.

"Their parents want my head. They say it's my fault. The kids don't like me."

"They like you fine. They just don't like school."

"Why won't they just arrest Roger? You said yourself he's taking the kids."

"I didn't say that. Plus, no one knows where he's taking them." I slink toward the wine bottle to see if she'll stop me. She doesn't.

"He hasn't done anything," I say, pouring a glass. "He doesn't hurt them."

"You don't know that."

"I'll try and do something, okay, Lovely? I will."

She cries on my shoulder, thanking me, but I have no idea what I'll do.

On Sunday, Duk is preaching in the nail salon. White women who had appointments storm out, but all the Korean men are in there now with their wives and families, just like it used to be.

I watch from outside with a pocket full of new kiwis, looking for Janet. There she is, sitting on a sink, head bowed. Her hair is black but shiny white in the salon's fluorescent lights.

Duk spots me midsermon through the window. He points, and the whole congregation turns as if I were just what he was talking about. There's violence in their Christian eyes. I take off, running.

Later that night on my walk back to the bushes, Janet is outside of the salon, putting packages into the basket on her bike. I walk up, presenting a kiwi, thinking, *Now is my chance*, but Roger's bus pulls in between us. Janet gets on, squealing, and Roger starts all the lights on the thing like it's a goddamn party.

I haven't tasted a kiwi yet and won't until it's with her. I pocket them again, though they are getting bruised. If only I had a refrigerator.

There are no kids in the lot at recess, just a few more cops milling around and taking notes. Everyone's either kidnapped by Roger or kept home by terrified parents. They realized Roger was just running the bus route five minutes ahead of schedule and picking up whoever was waiting. And the kids always got on.

With nothing to do, Clip and I rearrange the cones in the lot into the shape of a bus, hoping we might conjure the kids up. We've been overzealous again and become Wite-Out-painted Indians. Lovely sees what we've done and yells at us to go home, the school is closed, we may be fired.

"I'm sick of the bushes," Clip says that night, and all I can see of him are the white splotches under the moon. "Let's try the old Korean church tonight. We could sleep there, take a bath in leftover holy water. You wanna?"

We walk down to the church, and Clip breaks in.

"Why don't we do that to our apartment?" I ask him, not knowing he knew how to do that.

He just says, "Do what?"

Dim stained-glass saints line the walls in the church, angry in the dark. Clip runs to the pulpit and says, "A reading from the first letter to Clip. 'I think we should see other people. Amen.'" He pulls the ether out of his coat, uncorks it, saying, "Do this in memory of me," and takes a sniff. I approach the altar.

"Did you go to the nail salon?" I ask him.

"No. But Roger took me."

"In the bus?"

"Yup. He's after Janet, too."

"I noticed. Why?"

"Stupid question. He's the one she wants, too, sorry to say. That's the movie right there. See the difference?"

I don't. Roger is a kidnapper with a bus. I'm a huffer with a job.

"Roger's the dangerous guy her dad hates. She's the girl no one can have. You're just an extra who walks across the set every once in a while. It's best for us to wait this one out."

"But I think we're involved already."

"No, no," Clip says. "We have our own movie. The quest. The quest to find our keys!" Then he blesses me with more karate chops; we take the sacrament and fall asleep in the pews.

I ether-dream of Janet. The hard back of the wooden bench can't wake me, and it feels good sleeping here. I can smell her and her people, feel their god up on the wall, watching me back.

I know Roger. Premed or not, he knows nothing of my Janet's kiwis.

We oversleep, and Clip and I hear someone coming into the church in the morning. We run to one of the confessionals and hide.

It's Roger and the kids. They all file up the center aisle toward the altar and take seats in the pews. The kids' uniforms are untucked, but they are happy and well behaved.

"Now's our chance," I whisper, but Clip shakes his head.

"Let's see what happens."

"We're late for work."

"Doesn't look like they'll need us."

Roger walks up to the pulpit and drags a full human skeleton replica from one of the side vestibules toward center stage. The kids cheer. One of them yells, "Mr. Bad-to-the-Bone!"

Then Janet appears, dressed in her nail salon whites. A new shout goes up from the kids: "Nurse Miss Janet, Nurse Miss Janet!" She waves and bows a little.

Roger opens a briefcase from under the altar, dons a surgeon's mask, and places a microscope on the altar. Janet stretches rubber gloves, and he slips his hand in and kisses her on the forehead. She begins arranging test tubes in racks, and the children are buzzing in their pews. Then she places a syringe on a metal platter.

"So where were we yesterday?" Roger asks his congregation. "Anyone remember?"

A few kids yell back, "Blood types!"

"Good, good. That's right, blood types. I need a volunteer!"

Twenty hands go up.

Duk and the Koreans must have been doing their own detective work. Roger made a strange display of his crime, and it wouldn't be impossible to follow that bus.

As a few kids file up toward Roger and his needle, the Koreans burst through the front entrance of the church, running on their own short legs toward the altar.

Clip nods at me, like, *See?*

Roger and the Koreans struggle at the pulpit, and their shouts and blows echo in the empty church. The needle clatters on the marble. Kids start to cry.

The Koreans grab Roger, walk him down the aisle toward who-knows-where, but Duk stays behind the altar and a look flashes across his face like he's finally at home. He holds his hands out—both palms up—and begins to pray in Korean, holy sing and holy pow.

Watching all this happen, with the rafters of the church pointing up, the kids' cries ringing the windows like bells, the uncorked fumes in this booth, I feel moved to pray, to confess.

Kids, I would say, *I'm sorry for this monster. I'm sorry for ever taking medicine lightly. Lovely, I've sinned against your school; Duk, against your church. And Janet, I have confused things about you the most. Forgive me.*

Clip, on the other hand, says, "You know, we could just spill the rest of this gallon in here and stay gone for a couple days. I don't want to deal with any of this shit."

The moment is gone, so we lie back and don't watch, huffing a little, the sound going in and out like it does. I can hear Duk yelling at Janet and her sobbing. Eventually the bus starts outside and I get a whiff of its awful exhaust. We look out, and the church is finally empty.

"We can leave now," I say.

We creep out, and the saints are alive in the morning sunlight. Clip stops in front of one who's holding a staff and says, "I need one of those."

I'm not sure if Clip means a large wooden stick to coax sheep and crush snakes and part waters. Or a holy person like that to believe in and appeal to. I don't ask.

"What were we about to see?" I ask Clip. I'm thinking of the needle.

"No idea. Thank God we're not involved though, huh?"

Roger's bus is the Koreans' again. They just took it back. It says "Repent Sinners" on the side once more.

Roger has disappeared. There were no police involved that I know of. The Koreans didn't want it, out of shame. No one in the neighborhood ever mentioned the bus incident again—not the parents or the teachers. I think there's a great feeling of guilt about the whole thing, as if the town had created Roger out of its own nightmares and was somehow responsible.

The kids are sad. Lovely says that during art class, many of them draw buses and fight scenes in a church and happy-look-ing hospitals.

The Koreans permanently turn the nail salon into a church on Sundays, but Duk is happy. His congregation has returned, and though they have to sit on sinks and footbaths, they are devout once again. On the street, he's a stained-glass saint lit up in the sun. Birds land on his shoulders. He even performs a miracle and opens the door to our apartment.

"We had a deal," he says, as his nephew—a locksmith of all things—packs up his tools. We peek into the apartment, and our keys are hanging by the door, right where they belonged. They were never lost.

This Is Ambler

THE ASBESTOS FACTORY

MY FRIENDS AND I rented a house in Ambler, Pennsylvania, for a while. The town had once been called "the asbestos capital of the country," and the factory was still there like a giant tombstone. They must have been afraid to knock it down. Rumor was that asbestos used to roll through the streets in big, spiky tufts like tumbleweed. Rumor was that when the factory closed, they just buried what was left and built a playground on top of it.

We were juniors in college. Clip took a photography class and used the town of Ambler as subject matter. The Christian Cinema with its marquee announcing, "Hell Awaits." The grizzled ex–factory workers drinking beer and tomato juice at the Easy Street Pub. The hand-painted billboard that said "Stay Inspired!" as you drove out of town.

According to Clip, he had a solid B in the course but wanted the A. His other grades were not so hot. His final project was due soon.

"The factory," he said. "That's some A-plus shit, I bet."

He had his camera hanging around his neck like jewelry. It swung around and almost dipped into his coffee while he talked.

"When's the full moon?" I said. "Mood lighting."

"No," he said. "No, we want inside. We want *interiors*."

"'We'?" I said. "Like you-and-your-camera 'we'?"

"No," he said. "Me-and-you 'we.' I need someone to carry my equipment."

Clip and I walked up Main, toward the factory. The SEPTA train ran parallel with our street, and a small, flimsy fence tried to keep little kids and puppies off the tracks. The Dog Pound, a group of local teenage drug dealers, was not out on their usual corner that afternoon, but we crossed to the other side of the street anyway, out of habit. We called them the Dog Pound because at least one of them always had a pit bull on an enormous, thick chain. But it was early afternoon, and a weekday. The Dog Pound was probably still at high school.

"What if the factory is locked?" I said. "It's probably locked."

"We'll kick our way in, boss," Clip said. "This is high art! Nothing can stand in our way."

"Breaking and entering?" I said. "Is that worth the A?"

We'd had our run-ins with Ambler cops before. They seemed to resent our presence in town more than they did the drug dealers'. They showed up at every party we threw, while we shoved the minors into the basement. It was harassment, really. Our next-door neighbors were literally deaf. They would never have called the cops.

"The A is inconsequential," Clip said. "It's my duty as an artist."

I'd never heard Clip refer to himself as an artist before.

"Plus," Clip said, "in a foot race, we got this."

· · ·

The front door to the factory was open. Actually, there was no door anymore, just a frame. The floor was covered in rust and glass, so we crunched right in. The sun through the dust inside made the air inside the factory palpable, almost gave it a taste.

"Is that asbestos?" I said, pointing to the gold filaments floating in the air. I was carrying Clip's canvas equipment bag that tore a little with each step. I didn't know what was in it.

"They're just harmless motes of dust," Clip said. "Plus, it would take a lot to kill you. Hand me my light meter."

Where did Clip learn a word like "motes"? College, I guess.

I gave him what I thought he wanted, and he scraped it along the top of some fossilized machine. Dirt and crud and dead bugs fell to the ground, and then he pulled two forties from the bag and put them on top of the machine.

"When these are done," he said, "we're done. An artist needs a time limit. Can't overthink it."

I cracked my forty and took a big swig. I didn't want to stay long.

"Now then," Clip said, and cracked one himself. "Now *then*." He held the camera up to his eye and swigged his beer underneath it. "Beautiful."

He took pictures of old, beat-up shit. Chutes and compressors and valves that, I guess, would look cool in black-and-white with all the shadows. But who knew? He had no patience or skill in the darkroom. Clip was uninterested in the end result, but was genuinely obsessed by beautiful subject matter. It was as if he were staking out sites for better photographers. He was some kind of willing, aesthetic guinea pig.

I sat five feet from the door, drinking my forty, while Clip cataloged what he called the "filigrees" of light. College did this to some kids. You could never tell what the brain would retain. For Clip, it was this strange new vocabulary, though he barely had any idea how to use the equipment he had borrowed from the school. I tried to slow down my breathing so as not to take in so much asbestos.

"It feels good to breathe the rough stuff," Clip said, sucking the air now like through a straw. "The air pollution myth never hit me very hard. But now I get it."

"So it *is* asbestos?" I asked.

"It ain't, like, the fresh mountain air." Clip said. He reached in his bag and threw me a disposable camera. "Take a picture of me, boss," he said and puckered his lips again. I snapped and flashed the camera at him, spun the gear until it clicked, and then he smiled.

"Fantastic," he said. Clip was really at home in that factory.

Shit was falling from the ceiling now. Our footsteps were rattling old, rusted machinery loose. Bats woke and flew off to find a new place to sleep. A stray dog was disturbed, too, gave us a growl, but left to wander the train tracks.

Then Clip found a staircase that climbed a good twenty feet, very steep.

"Let's go up," Clip said. He took two steps at a time, his clang echoing through the huge room. I grabbed the bag and started up the stairs behind him. Rotted pieces of metal crumbled beneath our feet, but the structure held. It was hard climbing with that bag and our two forties.

The top floor of the factory was bright orange. The roof was half gone by then, and the setting sun lit up the rust-covered machinery. It was like someone just turned on all the color in the world.

It took us a couple of minutes to notice it, the glare was so bad and our eyes were adjusting. But it wasn't a miracle, and it wasn't the malt liquor. There was a dump truck up on the second floor of that factory. Clip snapped a picture of the truck right away, and then it started to sink in.

"How in the world did they get that up here?" Clip said.

There was no ramp, no elevator. No doorway wide enough to drive it through, even if we had been on the ground floor. It made no sense.

"We should go," I said, and pulled long on my forty, not sure if that was still part of the deal.

The truck was huge. Its tires were three feet high and still inflated. Its paint was this toxic kind of yellow. The cab and the payload were empty, thank God. Clip just stared.

"This floor's gonna give some day," Clip said. "Boom!"

"I'm going downstairs," I said. "Take the damn picture."

"It's like the truck is staring at us," Clip said. "Do you feel that way?"

"Not really," I said and went down the stairs.

Clip stayed on the top floor for a long time. I didn't want to leave him, but didn't want to climb back up those steps. I considered yelling for him, but thought my voice might cause some kind of avalanche. Instead, I just waited, away from where I thought the truck was overhead, and finished my beer.

Clip would get his A, I thought. He could barely aim and shoot his camera, but he had a knack for finding things like this.

Finally, he came down the steps with a big grin.

"Wow." he said. "Ready?"

"Get your shots?" I asked as we walked out into the parking lot.

"The shots," Clip said. "The shots were gotten." He wore his camera now on his back, like a cape. We started walking home. The attic of our house, trimmed in green paint, was visible even blocks away.

"It's amazing," Clip said, "that they let us rent that house. It's too big for us. We're just kids."

"The house is cool," I said.

Clip had found it for us and charmed the old Italian landlord into letting college kids rent it. He was right; it was a miracle. Some days we just stood around in the foyer and laughed. Laughed, even, about the word "foyer."

"I've been thinking, there's only two ways that they got that truck up there," Clip said. "Either a helicopter dropped it in through the roof, or they had some sort of enormous driveway that they've gotten rid of."

He took the last sip of his forty and seemed satisfied. He threw his bottle over the fence toward the train tracks.

"Think you'll get that A?" I asked.

He looked me in the eye. "Absolutely," he said.

We kept walking down our street. The low-level drug dealers were out on their corner now, glaring at us. Their pit bull barked. I stared at the ground, but Clip was out in space, deep in thought.

"Look out," I said. "Dog Pound in the house."

"I used to like that they were our neighbors," he said. "Now, I don't know. They don't do much for me. I guess they're not that interesting."

The Dog Pound cursed and laughed at us. By the end of that year, they would steal a lot of expensive stuff from our house. Kick in our doors, break windows, and get off scot-free, though everyone knew who did it. The Ambler cops would tell us it was probably someone who had been to one of our parties, a friend of ours. But none of that had happened yet.

The house two doors down from ours was a residential home for the mentally retarded. They hung out on the porch and howled and giggled. Each week, their trash had more empty beer cans than ours did. We joked sometimes that it was hard to tell their house from ours.

One of them yelped from the porch when we walked by, "Hello, losers! Hello!" Someone had taught them that word.

Clip waved. Usually, he'd give them the finger.

He walked up onto our porch and stopped.

"There's one other way they could have gotten that truck up there," he said. "Maybe they put it together, piece by piece, up on the second floor. What if that's what they did? Just built the thing up there?"

"Why would they do that?" I asked.

"Why? Because the factory was closing and they were dying and they wanted to fuck with people. Wanted people like me and you to see it."

"And do what?" I asked.

"I don't know," Clip said. "Feel weird. Wonder about them."

The Dog Pound was lighting M-80s in the street whenever a car stopped at their stop sign. The retards were singing along to their Beach Boys' Christmas album again. I didn't believe Clip's explanations for the dump truck. I knew there must be a simpler reason, one we couldn't know, one that made good sense. But still, I liked Clip's better.

"One day," Clip said, "that truck's gonna fall and then everyone will know. But until then—" He put his fingers to his lips. "Shh."

The sun was setting over the pond across the street. Actually, it was a swamp. It wasn't pretty, just goose crap and mosquitoes.

A SEPTA train banged by on its way to Philadelphia, not stopping at the station. Its horn blared. Its wheels screeched.

"This town used to be nice, I bet," Clip said. "Then they closed the factory, and everything went to shit."

"It happens," I said. I didn't know where he was going with this.

"I bet there's some old son of a bitch somewhere in this

town who wishes they never found out asbestos was bad," Clip
said. "What good came of that?"

"People stopped getting cancer," I said. Then I remembered
that our house, foyer and all, was probably still lined with that
poison.

Clip lit a smoke and said, "Cancer? What's that to an artist?"

THE AU PAIR

One Saturday night, Clip came home and said he'd met a girl
from New Zealand. None of us believed him. New Zealand
was far off.

He said she was an "au pair." We didn't know what it meant,
but he told us it meant she was a babysitter from another
country.

We said, "Sure she is."

During that first week, the phone rang, but we couldn't
understand what the voice on the line was saying. "Excuse
me?" we said, or "Huh?" if we were drunk.

Eventually, we figured out the voice wanted to talk to Clip.
We could make out his name, at least. We gave him the phone,
and he went up to his room in the attic and shut the door.

That was Michelle.

The next weekend, she showed up at the house. She had
long blond braids, green eyes. She was the most beautiful girl
who had ever been to our house. She had this accent like the
people who get attacked by sharks.

All four of us in the house went to college: some for rich
kids, some for poor kids. Milk went to one for stupid kids.
We dated American college girls, brainless psychology majors
mainly. Julies. We never cleaned up or anything if any of the
Julies were coming over. Someone would be in his underwear

at all times. If a Julie left a toothbrush in our bathroom, we'd throw it out the window.

But Michelle was different. We folded the afghan on the back of the couch when we knew she was coming. The vacuum howled. When she showed up, we all followed her around. She was an event. She wore these thin gypsy dresses, and you could see the outline of her underwear through them. And she didn't wear that much underwear.

Michelle said, "I only drink gin."

So we bought twenty-dollar gin. We hated gin.

She said, "College is for bourgeois money-fuckers."

We agreed and shut our books.

She sat cross-legged in our chairs, bouncing her knees. Her nipples were like two eyes that I was in a staring contest with.

Then Clip took her to his room in the attic. The roof up there was pointed like a steeple, and people would always bang their heads. The attic had no vents either, so it was always either freezing or sweltering. We liked both scenarios, thinking about her and her body sweating or pulled tight in the cold. When they went upstairs, the rest of us just huddled in the living room, not saying much, sipping our awful gin. The phone rang. Our American girlfriends were leaving messages we didn't feel like returning right then.

In the morning, Michelle cooked breakfast: awful pancakes made only of flour and water and salt. She wore one of Clip's T-shirts like some kind of teddy bear while she stood over the stove. The leftover smell of her perfume or shampoo wafted down from the night before, but also something else. Her morning breath, the sweat between her legs, a cigarette she had already smoked that morning. It made me hungry.

We ate her pancakes and asked her question after question, just to hear her talk.

She said, "The kids I take care of are so spoiled. I want to tie them up and torture them."

Warren asked, "Do you have to give them baths?"

I thought that was a good question. I liked thinking about that.

She said, "They can't even decide which room to watch television in."

Milk asked, "Does the toilet flush the other way down there?"

That one wasn't as good. She had nothing to do with toilets, in my mind.

Clip just sat in a chair drinking coffee, shoveling pancakes. He always looked worn out in the mornings.

"These are terrible," he said and laughed.

One night, Michelle wanted to play Ouija. It took us a while to understand what she was suggesting with her accent and everything, but then we agreed. We were drinking gin again. We were starting to like it. I liked mine with Sprite.

Michelle wrote out the alphabet on a piece of paper, along with the words "yes" and "no." She told us someone should take a cup from the cabinet, go outside, and ask a spirit to come into the cup. It was one a.m.

I took the cup outside and held it up. It was cold out there. I sincerely asked the spirit to come into the glass and then went back inside. I wanted to impress Michelle. We held the cup above the letters for a long time, everyone trying to get his fingers to touch hers. We asked, "Are you there? Are you there?"

Nothing happened. The cup wouldn't even move to the word "no."

Michelle said, "We're too drunk. The spirits don't like it when we're this drunk."

We quit the game and drank more. Clip tugged on Michelle's braids. She put one in her mouth and bit down on it.

I went to my room. My heart hurt. But when I was brushing my teeth, some books fell off of my bookshelf. The spirit had moved them, I thought.

When I went downstairs to tell everyone, Michelle was in the bathroom, getting sick.

She said, "I hate gin. I hate gin."

Clip could not get her off of the floor. He said, "She said she could outdrink us Americans." He chuckled.

Michelle started to cry. "You're just schoolboys!" she said.

It took Clip a long time to get her up the steps to the attic. The rest of us stood around and watched. When he shut the door, we went to bed.

The next morning there was no breakfast. I got up around eleven and made coffee. None of us usually ate breakfast anyway. The Ouija board was still on the table, and I remembered I never got to tell anyone about the spirit that had moved the books in my room. Something was at work. Michelle showered for half an hour, and I milled around in my room, hoping to get a glimpse of her. Finally, she came out, wrapped in a towel that was too small. Her breasts were packed and bursting. She left hot little footprints as she walked up the steps to the attic. She smiled at me. It was obvious what I was doing.

Clip stood at the top of the steps in the doorway to the attic. He looked at me and smacked Michelle on the butt as she walked past. There was no hot water left when I got in the shower.

We didn't see Michelle during the week because of her job taking care of those kids. Clip told us she was going to be sent back to New Zealand soon if she didn't improve. Her au pair family wasn't happy with her.

He said, "She tells the parents their kids are fat. One of the

kids started a fire in the backyard. They're gonna trade her in,
I think."

"Do you have to marry her?" Milk asked.

"I don't want to," Clip said. "She wants to live here. I told
her no way. You guys wouldn't have it."

Milk and I grimaced at Clip. I'm not sure why Milk made
that face, but I know why I made it. Clip was wrong.

"Where would she sleep?" Milk asked. We all had our own
ideas.

Michelle came over the next weekend. She didn't seem very
happy. She and Clip had had many long conversations on the
phone that week, but she was dressed in an evening gown
when she rang the doorbell. A small diamond lay in the divot
between her clavicles, and her blond braids had been twisted
onto the top of her head in a fancy way.

She saw my surprise and said, "We have to go to the orchestra tonight."

I remembered that Clip's parents had given him two tickets
to the performance, an out-of-town collection of musicians.
Clip had always been a music lover. Or, rather, a lover of the
rooms crafted to play music in—auditoriums, amphitheaters.
He studied the physics of it. It was part of the reason he chose
to live in our misshapen attic.

Clip came downstairs in a suit. I had never seen this. He
looked good.

"The orchestra," I said, and he nodded. Warren had just
gone to buy forties. But it made sense to take a girl from New
Zealand someplace exotic.

They left, and the rest of our girlfriends came over. We
drank malt liquor and played with the gin-stained Ouija
board. It told me that I would have three kids, and then told

my Julie that she was infertile, actually spelled the word out.

In front of our girls, we started to make fun of Michelle.

Warren said, "Her pancakes! God, they're made of puke."

We tried her accent but couldn't get it right.

Milk said, "Why doesn't she make some koala bacon? That, I'd eat."

We kept drinking until the girls passed out. We were waiting for Clip and Michelle to get back. We talked differently once the girls were snoring.

Warren said, "Clip's gonna dump her, the dumb bastard. I can tell. He's got that look."

I said, "You should have seen her dressed up."

Milk said, "And she could drink"—he pointed to our girls—"better than these."

It got to be one a.m. We started to worry. The orchestra did not go all night.

Finally, before two, the front door slammed, and the three of us rushed into the front room. Michelle looked like she had been crying before, but was definitely mad now. Clip was smiling. He walked into the kitchen and opened a beer.

"Mind if I have one? Who bought these?"

We heard Michelle stomp the steps to the attic. Our girlfriends woke up. They went to the attic to check on Michelle.

"How was it?" I asked.

"Michelle cursed at the woman next to us because she was wearing a chinchilla coat. Called her a 'bourgeois animalfucker.' The acoustics in there were amazing, though. You could hear every fuckup."

The auditorium was new. I wondered if it was like those old amphitheaters where you could hear a pin drop on stage from way up in the nosebleeds.

"So did everyone hear?" I asked. I was a little drunk.

"No. The woman couldn't even understand her. Her stupid accent."

Clip finished his beer and opened another. He didn't seem in a hurry to get back to Michelle. Upstairs, the bathroom door slammed.

Our girlfriends came back down. They were half awake and half drunk. They were ugly. Milk's girl looked fatter than usual. Warren's had a big crease mark on her face from sleeping on the couch.

"What did you guys do tonight?" Clip asked, even though it seemed pretty obvious.

My Julie said, "Can we go to sleep now?" I ignored her and she went back to the sofa with the other girls. "You should go up there, Clip. She's upset."

"I'll go," I said. My girl glared at me.

"It's okay," Clip said. "I'll go in a minute."

He started describing a woman in the orchestra. "She had a big violin. A cello. And her big fat legs were wrapped tight around that thing. I couldn't stop staring at her."

He saw we didn't understand. Milk swayed into the fridge with a thump.

"She had this look on her face, and the bow was going, and it was so deep and loud. You could feel it in like your—I don't know." We thought he was going to say something dirty, but instead he said, "The look on her face was like she was skydiving or something. Like someone dropped her out of her airplane."

"She was good?" I asked.

"She was pretty good," Clip said.

"You're gonna dump her, aren't you?" Warren asked.

Clip wiped his mouth. "Probably. Fucking babysitter."

A few minutes passed. It was quiet upstairs. The girls were snoring again on the couch.

"Watch this," Clip said, and put his beer on the oven.

He walked into the living room and started tying the girls' shoelaces together. When we saw what he had in mind, we helped.

Clip didn't like girls so much as he liked the ruckus they could make. He didn't dump Michelle in any official way. He knew she was going to have to go home soon, and he looked forward to it. Not to her being gone, but to the time just before she left. He could be cruel.

We didn't see Michelle again. Clip talked about her as if she were a million miles away. Sometimes the phone would ring and we'd look at him and he'd say, "Nah. It's like three a.m. in New Zealand." There was something about him, like he sent her there.

He brought a new girl back to the house after a few weeks. Her face was already raw from making out with Clip in the car. He had a bit of a beard coming in. He told her he liked gin and made her a drink.

Clip's new girl told us she wanted to be a stripper. We weren't impressed. She was a freshman with bobbed brown hair. She looked like the rest of our girlfriends.

Clip said, "There's a strip club up the street if you want a job," and the girl got quiet. It was true. We'd been there. She took off her sweater and her T-shirt said, "Eat me."

"Put your sweater back on," Clip said. "Don't be stupid." He'd already told us she was an ice cube in bed.

We played the Ouija game again. Clip's girl giggled from the gin. She would puke soon, we could tell. Clip was making her drinks too strong. He did this on purpose. There would be no breakfast.

When I took the cup outside to ask for the spirit, I thought of Michelle. I sincerely asked her to come into the cup. We all wanted her to.

Inside, Clip had already taken his new girl upstairs. The rest of us hovered above the board and asked, "Are you there? Are you there?"

The cup rattled and then slid to "no."

THE MOVE OUT

After our house was robbed a second time, we knew something was up. A break-in was one thing, but two felt more like an insult. The first time we were robbed, they only took what they could carry. An Xbox, some DVDs, Warren's coffee can full of loose change. It had actually taken us a few days to notice everything that was missing. We didn't call the police. At first, we blamed each other. Was our copy of *Goodfellas* lost at some girlfriend's apartment? Had someone needed change for laundry and taken Warren's without asking? We were used to this sort of bickering in the house. And it was packed with so much junk.

But on the second break-in, it seemed that the thief had brought his friends. And maybe one of those friends had a pickup truck. Clip's and Warren's guitars were gone, and Clip's Orange cabinet amp. Whole rows of movies and games from the shelves. Roger's grandfather's watch. My telescope and my skateboard. The back door—a flimsy piece of particleboard anyway—was cracked off of its hinges, and the doorknob lay on the floor. I mean, it was obvious.

Days afterward, we were still discovering that things were missing. It was a weird feeling. Anything I didn't have on hand and hadn't thought about in a few days could potentially be gone. Each night, I'd drive back to the house from work, running through a checklist of things I remembered that I owned. My autographed '85 Phillies baseball. Some nude Polaroids of my psychology-major girlfriend. The Swiss Army knife my father had given me. Could these be gone, too?

It was Bad Times in the Ambler house all around. We had all graduated in May with useless liberal arts degrees. We preferred a "classical education," but maybe we had just spent four years avoiding things like math and mornings. By July, out on our own in the big, bad world, we were miserable.

For instance:

Clip decided, at the age of twenty-two, to start smoking cigarettes because it was the only thing to do at his job. He worked as a production assistant at a reggae studio in the suburbs of Philadelphia called Jah Rasta. Recording music was his passion, but he hated this particular genre—said it sounded like the circus—and hated the clientele even more. Low-level thugs faking Jamaican accents, getting high and saying, "What the blood clot?" to each other over and over. They never recorded anything. Sometimes he was even paid in weed, a drug none of us liked, but a drug he'd also smoke in his room in the attic, again out of boredom. And so Clip developed a pretty nasty cough.

Warren was the only nonhandicapped employee staffing the local liquor store. His fellow staffers were creepy men with knit square-bottom ties, or withered fingers, or cinder blocks for feet. They asked constantly to be invited to one of our parties. Nice guy that Warren was, he always gave them hope but never our address. But sensitive guy that he was, Warren was depressed by the place, the line waiting for him to open in the morning, the poison selling. He refused to bring anything home from the store but empty boxes.

Roger was working on a nearby farm and was actually screwing the farmer's sixteen-year-old daughter in places like "the barn." The rest of us had never been in a barn, thought they didn't make them anymore. He could go to jail. Plus, all his DUIs. He had been trained as an oil painter, so he painted pigs and wheat and naked women in his room until all hours. He insisted on using the toxic John Deere green with the door and windows in his bedroom shut. He'd stagger out of his room to the bathroom as if he'd been sniffing ether in a cartoon.

I was selling the shit out of *The Secret Life of Bees* and *Who Moved My Cheese?* at Barnes & Noble. I'd argue whether it was "Harper Lee" or "Lee Harper" at least twice a week. I answered the question "Where is the nonfiction section?" over and over. I learned to gift-wrap things shaped like rectangles pretty well. In college, I had learned to feel the finer feelings with Wordsworth and Shelley and Bukowski. And now, all in all, I'd probably stolen five grand worth of books from the store.

We all had college degrees. Wasn't that the goal? We thought we were talented. We thought we were smart. But the rest of the world was shaking its finger and saying, "Not so fast . . ."

After the second robbery, Clip called the police and one came over finally. He pointed to the ruined back door and said, "There's your entry point." Then he paced around our kitchen and living room for a while as if he were looking for clues.

"So what do we do now?" Clip said. "We have lists of the stuff that was taken. A few serial numbers."

The cop laughed. "I've been here before," he said, looking toward the ceiling like he was taking the scent of something. He snapped out of it. "If I were you, I'd stop having all those parties." Ambler was not a big place. I guess we had a reputation. "All those people, in and out of here. All this nice stuff," he said as he walked past the two wheelchairs and the baby carriage we kept parked in the den. "Pretty tempting."

We had not stolen the carriage and wheelchairs. We found them. In the abandoned asbestos factory. It wasn't like there was some single mother in Ambler carrying her baby around all day with cramped arms. Or a bunch of cripples lying in the street like, *Thief! Thieves!* Was he blaming us for having cool stuff?

Clip forced the list on the cop, and he pocketed it. He put his hat on. "I'll let you know if we come up with anything, but I wouldn't hold your breath." He looked at Warren, who was the most seriously rattled by all this. "Or yours."

So Clip called Frank, our Italian landlord, and he came over with dead bolts for the front and back door. It took him four hours to install them. All that cursing in Italian. He didn't replace the back door, but instead hammered more plywood over where it had been booted in. We stood around, shaking our heads. It looked like the sort of solution we would have come up with ourselves.

Clip said, "What about an alarm system?"

Frank said, "Dead bolt good, Charley." He had never learned our real names, but after three years of living in the house, Clip was definitely "Charley." He slid the bolt in and out of place like he was explaining to us how it worked. "Ah," he said. "Click, click. At night. Safe, safe." For some reason we had expected an apology, a discount, something, but he acted like he had just fixed our garbage disposal. He whistled on his way out. They couldn't steal the house itself, so I guess he wasn't worried.

Then Clip called the local pawnshops, hoping to find his Gibson SG and Warren's Fender Precision. Would they be dumb enough to pawn it here in Ambler? I went with Clip to one of these shops. When he saw that their guitars were not there, he spent a lot of time looking at guns.

We worked through our list of suspects over pasta and forties. Each of us leaned toward a different culprit. Roger suspected the home for the mentally challenged two doors down, citing how brazen the crime was. "In broad daylight they robbed us," he said. "You'd have to be retarded to do that." But it seemed more and more that they couldn't have been *that* stupid. Because here we were—they got away with it. Twice. But any chance Roger had to insult people, he'd take.

I blamed the Man in Navy Blue, a mysterious figure always dressed in a navy jumpsuit, and almost always across the street when I came out on the porch. Could he always be either going to or coming from work at some mysterious garage? "He's been watching the house," I said. "He knows our cars. Whenever he sees me, he pretends he's doing calisthenics, like he's taking a break from jogging." But the Man in Navy Blue was thin and sickly looking, probably not able to move so much equipment in a short time. He was a crazy but probably not a criminal.

Clip blamed Roger's high school friends Raisin and Jerome. The rest of us didn't know them well, and they'd been spending a lot of time at the house with Roger on his days off. They'd all drink vodka and lemonade and play Xbox in marathon events. They'd stop only to get more lemonade, and by three in the afternoon all three would be incomprehensible. Even Roger only halfheartedly defended them.

"No more fucking guests," Clip said. "Those kids need to get their own bathroom to do drugs in." But why would Raisin and Jerome ruin a good thing? They both lived with their parents and drank *our* vodka and played *our* Xbox. What would be the point?

Finally, Warren said what we were all thinking but reluctant to say: "It's the Dog Pound." Those rogue high schoolers that ran the corner the next block up. No one had a "but" for this suggestion. We all just sighed and went to opposite corners of the house.

· · ·

Warren and I had had a run-in with the Dog Pound a few weeks before that was starting to make more and more sense. We had been walking home from the Ambler train station, and it was one in the morning. We had gone to see this band we liked, the Rattlesnakes, play in Philadelphia. As we walked down Butler toward the house, we saw that the Dog Pound was out on their corner. They laughed and pointed their forty bottles at us from a distance. They were just high school kids, but when they were drunk, they were dangerous. One held a pit bull on a piece of chain. One was smoking a Backwoods, his hands buried in his pockets. One flipped the hood of his sweatshirt up over his ball cap and started toward us, his forty in his hand behind him like a tail standing straight up. It wasn't out of the question that one of them had a cracked, secondhand pistol.

"Hey, hey, it's the Monkees," the hooded one said. As he got closer, we saw the patchy goatee that was curling around his mouth. A turned canine tooth stuck out between his lips. We knew this guy. We'd been calling this one "Fang."

It was a comment we'd heard before. All of us in the house had decided to grow ironic, shaggy haircuts that year. We were going for Mick Jagger, John Lennon, but really we were Micky Dolenz or, worse, Rod Stewart. We held our hands up: *Good joke, you got us.* We kept walking.

"Your show is fucking stupid," another one said. "Bunch of fags running away from girls." He blew smoke at us that smelled like weed and cherries. They weren't usually this aggressive.

"Dude, shut up," Fang said. "They really are in a band. I hear them practicing. Hey, what's your band called?"

"The Monkees," Warren said. I wished he hadn't. It wasn't even funny.

"Fuck you. For real. I want to buy a CD." He reached in his pocket and pulled out a wad of cash.

"Don't worry about it," Warren said.

"What? We're not cool enough?" He started to cross the street, his hands out at his sides like an aggressive sort of shrug. The other two followed. I wanted to run.

These kids had always made me nervous. They were too stupid—too drunk or high—to be trusted. And they were in a mood that night. Something had gone wrong for them earlier, something that they were about to take out on us.

Just then a car pulled up at the corner, and the Dog Pound got distracted. Fang lowered his ball cap further over his eyes, and the other two began scanning up and down the street, puffing clouds of dope like a smoke screen. Future business majors. They had forgotten us just like that.

A month after the second robbery, I came home from work with a bag full of books I'd stolen about cosmology and Christian martyrs. I was very democratic, still liberal about my arts. But I didn't read many of the books I took. Not yet. I told myself I was building a library for some time in the future, when I had money, and children, and leisure. And bookshelves.

It was after midnight, and the whole house was up. This wasn't that strange, but there was no party. Clip, Warren, and Roger were just leaning in the kitchen. A pot of coffee was brewing.

"Where were you?" Clip said, but my store name tag was still hanging around my neck. It was pretty obvious.

"The fucking orchestra," I said. "What's going on?"

Warren's face was red and splotchy, like he'd been crying. Clip's hand was cut up. Roger was grinning in a bad way. I put the books down and scanned the house. Things seemed in order.

"It's like *Poltergeist*," Warren said.

"What is?" I said. No one was filling me in.

"This house. The way it's *ejecting* us."

"That's a haunted house, boss," Clip said. "This place isn't haunted. It's just really easy to break into."

"Maybe it's built on an Indian burial ground," Warren said. "Remember the Ouija board? Maybe the spirits are angry."

"The Indians don't want your Xbox and porno magazines," Clip said.

"I wouldn't mind having them," Roger said. We all stopped. We'd known Roger a long time, but sometimes he said these sorts of things. He was forever unhelpful. And he hadn't had much stolen himself. "Look, Warren had it right before," he said. "It's the Dog Pound. You guys know it, and I know it." He walked across the kitchen with his back to the rest of us, pulled himself up on the door frame to the living room, and swung like a monkey for a minute. Letting it sink in, I guess. "We need to go over there," he said to the empty room.

The robbed room. When I looked past him, I saw the shattered window, the emptied DVD shelf. The missing speakers and empty entertainment center. Even our fish tank had been pulled over, and the carpet was still soaked and bubbling, the fish long flushed. Just the two ratty couches pointed at the blank wall, like, *Are we next?*

No one drank coffee that night. Instead, we each went to our bedrooms and the house was strangely quiet. No music, no hum of TV, no murmurings to psychology major girlfriends. We were listening.

Before, I think we thought of the robbery like lightning, only striking once, a destructive but interesting event. But that wasn't the right metaphor. And it was really embarrassing that we liberal arts guys couldn't come up with the right metaphor.

Warren was spooked. He didn't believe in ghosts but thought the situation was beyond his understanding. I got that. Roger was looking for a fight, and I understood that, too. Clip was relying on things like police, justice, insurance paperwork. He was expecting a check for his missing equipment. He was researching what to buy. I was the only nostalgic one in the group. My things were not nice, but they were mine. Stealing the telescope I never used did hurt me. I was saving it. And it was a gift.

The house where we thought Fang, the leader of the Dog Pound, lived was on the street perpendicular to ours. We could even see the back of the house from ours, and had watched Fang and his friends working on cars and blaring bad music for the past three years. It made sense. They would have heard the guitars, seen our cars coming and going from the lot out back, too. Fang's house was a lot like ours — much too big and old for a traditional family to live in. Clip and Roger banged on the front door while Warren and I stayed farther down the steps. An old woman answered the door. She was drying her hands in a small kitchen towel.

"Ma'am," Clip said, "our house has been robbed a number of times in the past few months. The big green-and-white one around the corner. And we're asking around the neighborhood to see if any one has seen anything suspicious."

It was very neutral, what Clip said, very sensible. I had been expecting more anger and accusations, but I guessed that wasn't the best way at it. The woman looked at the four of us and then smiled in a mournful sort of way. Like Clip's question was cute.

"No," she said finally. "I haven't."

"Maybe your grandson?" Roger said. "Is he around?"

"I'm sorry to hear about the burglaries, but my grandsons live in West Orange, New Jersey," she said. Then she just kept drying her hands and waited for us. We all looked at each other.

"Well, the kids that go in and out of this house," Clip said. "Are they around?"

"I have no grandchildren in this house," she said. "Now, go on."

We could hear a ruckus being shushed behind her. A mean-sounding dog barked. Roger started to say something, and Clip grabbed his arm. A police cruiser drove by and slowed to a stop as we turned to go back home.

"Selling Girl Scout cookies?" the cop said. It was the same one who'd been to the house before.

"Her grandkids are stealing our stuff," Clip said. He walked up to the car and folded his arms. "Maybe you knew that, boss."

"Mrs. King's grandkids live in West Orange, Dick Tracy," the cop said. "Leave her alone."

"Yeah, we should get home," Roger said. "Someone is probably robbing our house right now." He tapped the back of the cruiser with his fist as he walked by and then lit a cigarette.

The cop threw the cruiser in park and got out. "Look here," he said. He was a huge man in a uniform a size too small, muscles bulging under pulled-tight gray cotton. Inside our house, on our turf, he hadn't seemed so scary. "Maybe you guys aren't getting the hint, but I think your college-boy vacation here is over." He backed Roger up against the cruiser's trunk. He looked like he might hit him.

"Like 'this town ain't big enough for the five of us'?" Clip said.

"That's right, professor," the cop said. "And I'm the sheriff."

"I call 'Indian'!" Roger said and began dancing and hooting. He pointed to Warren and me. "You're a pirate. You're an astronaut."

We all smiled. Mixed metaphors. Roger laughed more and brushed past the cop.

Warren looked above all of our heads and said, "It's really annoying that no one will help us. Aren't people supposed to help?" We were all a little frozen by Warren's complaint. It was genuine, but it was also ridiculous.

Finally, Clip looked back at the cop and said, "See you at high noon then, I guess." He wasn't smiling.

"Now it's funny?" the cop said. "Okay. Yuk it up. I don't want to hear about this again." He got back in his car, tugged on his siren, and drove off. I hated Ambler then. The asbestos. The lying grandmothers and the blame-the-victim cops. The Dog Pound who were making better career moves than we were. The confounding Man in Navy Blue. When we first moved in, we thought we had stumbled on some secret. But now, yeah, we got the hint. And for a second, it even seemed possible that Clip might shoot and kill that cop tomorrow.

When we got back to the house that afternoon, a mangy puppy was lying on a couch in our bare living room. It wagged its tail at us. It was thrilled we were there.

"A dog broke in?" Warren said. "Wonderful. I'm moving out."

"Me, too," Roger said as he scratched behind the dog's ear. "This place isn't safe."

Clip looked at me. "Well?"

"Screw it," I said.

Clip said, "Fine. The dog is mine though."

That was it. The end of Ambler. There was no showdown with the sheriff, though I did spend a lot of time imagining a shadowy Clip standing in the street, his hand hovering above his hip where his pawnshop gun was stashed, the wind off of the swamp we called Lake Ambler blowing trash between him and the cop like tumbleweeds. Who would draw first? Who had the best shot? But when I looked out the window at high noon the next day, all I saw was the Man in Navy Blue, stretching and jogging in place, and so I went back to packing.

On the last day, when we looked back at the house, it did not shrivel and collapse like the house in *Poltergeist*. There were no rising souls of the Indian dead. The house stood strong like a three-story headstone. But not even. The metaphor was off again. What would we be mourning? We wished for some moment of hilarity from the retards, or violence from the Dog Pound. Nothing happened. It was just an old house that might hold our smells and dents for a little. Better people could use the house for better things.

Clip did keep the dog. He threw its collar and tags in the trash and renamed it King Kong. A kind of revenge against the town. They would not get their puppy back. He moved back in with his dad, and would bring King Kong to the recording studio with him during the week. The Rasta guys really dug the puppy; his dad never mentioned it. When I asked him if he ever did buy a gun from the pawnshop, he told me, "Nope." When I asked him why he named the dog King Kong, he told me, "Because he's a badass." He still smokes too much.

Roger found a house with Raisin and Jerome in Ardsley and started painting what he called "stolen still-lifes": knocked-over bowls with half-eaten fruit on the table, shattered glass, empty bookshelves. They were very pretty. He sold a few of them for a lot of money. He bought a PlayStation 3 for their new house. Sometimes, I still think Roger knew more about what was going on than he said. He'd asked me to move into Ardsley, and I said no. I did go to a party there once, and thought about what I'd steal. It would have been easy.

Warren quit the liquor store and moved in with his psychology major girlfriend, though I guess she was a bartender then. She'd been duped just like the rest of us. I got Warren a job at the bookstore, and I showed him how to steal books. I told him the sensors were fake. I told him to just put the books in a bag like you bought them and walk out the front door. He had no interest. He said, "The last thing I need is more books." Two months later, he was teaching *The Catcher in the Rye* and *The Scarlet Letter* at Cardinal Dougherty.

I moved back into my parents' house in Fox Chase. They were glad to have me, and my room and all its stuff were exactly the way I left it. They smiled to each other as I carried in boxes full of books I've never read. At dinner, they told me about the neighborhood: who had gotten a hip replaced or bought a lemon of a car, who got a scholarship to high school and who was probably on drugs, who sold their house to a Korean family and who refused. So much news in Fox Chase.

But like everything else that happened in Ambler, I didn't tell my parents a thing about the robberies. Instead, I told them that we had each decided it was time to move on, to grow up. I had a hundred and fifty dollars saved up, and would have my own place in no time. No one was going to give us anything anymore, right? We had to go out and take it. My parents were very proud.

This Is Recession

L IKE A LOT OF people who adopt dogs, Clip was in need of rescue himself. He chose a dog that seemed to come from the longest line of mutts. It was a dog only in the sense that it barked and panted and wagged. There might have been goat or bear in its genes. It walked on four legs, had a snout. Eventually, it ate dog food.

I went with Clip on the day he picked it up. Clip was very proud. He had scoured the cages at the shelter for a few weeks and finally made a decision. The staff at the shelter reviewed his application for thirty seconds and accepted it. He signed the paperwork and paid his eighty bucks. I thought, *Eighty bucks? That's a lot of charity.*

In the parking lot, he held the puppy up and fully appreciated that it had a penis.

"There's only one name for this dude," Clip said. "*King Kong.*"

King Kong sat in my lap as Clip sped home. King Kong cried the entire time.

"He liked his cage, I guess," I said. "He's kicking and biting me." The dog was not happy. It was, like, chirping. "He's part bird," I said.

"He doesn't know what he's in for," Clip said. "Big-time happy puppy party."

Clip stopped at the grocery store, and I waited in the car with this young life. I told it, "Welcome to the big show!" I said, "You're free. This is the greatest country in the world." But King Kong had buried himself under the seat, so I sent a few text messages.

I was waiting to hear about a job, and I had this superstitious way of thinking about my phone. I guess I thought about it like a dog. If I paid it enough attention, it would reward me with affection. But my phone wouldn't vibrate.

Forty-five minutes later, Clip returned with a T-bone, a bag of dog food, two plastic bowls, and a gallon of bright-blue Gatorade.

"Planning on exercising?" I said. "Need your electrolytes?"

"It's for King Kong," Clip said. "Gatorade is like penicillin for dogs." He scratched the dog's head, and the car veered onto the shoulder. "I Googled it," he said, and we got back on the road.

Clip *was* in need of rescue. Nothing was going right for him. Times were tough.

For instance: He had a kidney stone he was waiting to pass in pain. He was becoming strange. He'd call me into the bathroom and point to the toilet. "Now that color is just not natural," he'd say. He ate fourths of Percocet all day in expectation of this event. "Punch me," he'd say. "I can't feel it."

For instance: His student loan lender had finally tracked him down and sent two Persian thugs in soccer jerseys to his apartment to suggest he refinance. Clip blamed the bad economy, but he was spooked. He worked for a company called Clean Water Now! He went door-to-door, scaring housewives with a jar of murky water he claimed was from their source. But donations were down, and his hippie bosses were now acting very corporate.

For instance: Two of Clip's girlfriends had found out about each other when he took a third who was better at going through his cell phone's history. He referred to this event as "Julie-Gate" and didn't start many sentences after that without saying something like "Well, before Julie-Gate . . ." or "If Julie-Gate has taught me anything . . ." The girls had actually teamed up against Clip, putting aside their differences to get revenge. They had spray-painted "Untrustworthy" on one side of his car. On the other, they wrote "Insincere." When he saw the car, he said, "Well, that's not entirely true."

Clip drove a used Toyota Aptitude. The guy he bought the car from had claimed that it was a prototype that never made it to the States. He said the name of the car was a poor translation of how the Japanese kick ass in things like math. I said, "Isn't it the Chinese who are good at math?" but Clip ignored me. The car had its own set of problems. There was a sweet spot on the passenger side floor that turned off the electrical system. Greenish smoke puffed from the exhaust pipe. The trunk wouldn't open, but we could hear something roll around every time he stopped at a red light.

It was not in Clip's nature to admit defeat, but surely he was feeling defeated. And so: King Kong.

Clip let the dog run free as soon as we got it back to his apartment. He had not puppy-proofed the place. In fifteen minutes' time, King Kong destroyed four pillows from the couch, emptied three trash cans, pissed in two rooms, and chewed through one electrical wire. This last bit of destruction ended his reign of terror because he received a mild shock. Finally, King Kong lay down on the carpet and caught his breath. Clip thought this was all hysterical. "Don't touch that," he said to me, laughing. "That cord is still sparking."

Then Clip put a pan on the stove top and laid the T-bone in it. "This will teach him to love," he said. As the steak began to cook, King Kong rose up from the carpet in the living room and walked into the kitchen. "See?" Clip said. "He can't bear to be away from me." King Kong settled on the linoleum.

In the fluorescent light of the kitchen, I got a better look at the dog. It was drooling because of the steak and panting because of the chaos it had just caused. Its fur was brown and gray and black all at the same time. It had ears like a bat.

"He has ears like a bat," I said. "Maybe he's blind."

"All dogs are basically blind," Clip said. "But he can smell your mood."

King Kong looked at me. My mood was fine for the moment. I was enjoying watching Clip play mother to this animal. I had never seen him cook before.

"That steak smells good. Should I set the table?" I said. I pointed to the air hockey table in Clip's kitchen. King Kong got up and sniffed my ankles. I said, "See? I'm happy. I'm friendly. I'm feeling even keel."

Clip flipped the steak, and the new sizzle from the pan caught the dog's attention. It walked closer to the stove top and lay back down.

"I feel really good about this," Clip said. He scratched the dog's head. "This is exactly what we needed."

When King Kong was finished with the T-bone, he threw up in the living room and then ate the vomit. Clip said, "Well, that was easy." The dog began to snore, and so Clip turned the volume up on the TV. Two men in suits were discussing the economy. The graphics at the bottom of the screen read: "The Big Bailout: How It Affects You!"

"Shut up a minute," Clip said. "I want to hear this." I hadn't been talking.

Clip had never once discussed an issue with me that did not involve himself directly, so I thought this was noteworthy. He was taking an interest in global affairs.

"The problem was that there was no transparency in the credit default swap market," Clip said. "It was totally unregulated."

"Does the dog need to go out?" I said.

"Leverage is out the window," Clip said. He shook his head as if he had predicted this turn of events. I felt the need to chime in.

"To what extent was Julie-Gate a contributing factor to this current crisis?" I said. I was trying to get the conversation back to familiar territory. Girls and money—surely there was a connection.

He took the bait. "Julie always wanted me to get a dog," he said. "I should call her. She would be so pissed." I wasn't sure which Julie he was referring to, but I liked the idea. The men in suits on the TV were boring me. They were making Clip boring, too.

He didn't budge, though. He kept staring at the TV, and King Kong was still sleeping. The men in suits were discussing the "paper market." I assumed this was about recycling newsprint, but instead they spoke about banks lending to banks. Why would they do that? And every time someone I knew wore a suit, they were going to court or marrying someone they shouldn't. I nudged King Kong with my foot to try to get something going.

The dog grunted and stretched. It yawned and rose.

"He looks bigger," I said. "That steak and that nap really did something."

"Blue Gatorade," Clip said. He walked to the kitchen and poured the dog a bowlful. The dog followed and drank.

When Clip came back to the living room, those particular men in suits were gone. The topic changed to war. The topic changed to health care. The topic changed, and Clip wasn't interested. He turned the TV off and got down on all fours. King Kong bounded into the room. His feet were gigantic. He wanted to play.

Let me say that the economy was on my mind, too. I was unemployed. I had sold off my CDs and books and Indian arrowheads, and that had paid my rent and Internet the past month or so, but this sort of personal recycling was drying up. I had applied for a job that involved tailing newspaper delivery trucks to see if they were actually making their rounds. I applied for a job inserting pharmaceutical patents into a scanner. I applied to drive an ice cream truck. I had a college degree. So when I found out that the government was going to bail out the banks, I said something like, "Well, that's just great." I chanted "Main Street!" like everyone else. But I had never assumed that any bank would approve me for a loan. I guess I had been wrong. Honestly, this whole crisis seemed like a missed opportunity for me. I should have bought a house and gotten a couple credit cards.

Clip was playing with the dog. "Did you get a credit injection?" he said in a high-pitched voice as he tugged on King Kong's ears and legs. "Did you?" The dog was nipping at his hands and wagging its tail. This moment was interesting for a couple of reasons.

"So you *bailed out* King Kong?" I said. "I get it now."

"This dog is not a metaphor," Clip said. "He's a human life."

"Well," I said. The dog barked because Clip stopped playing.

"You know what I mean," he said. "The dog is not a bank. I'm not the Treasury Department. What would be the point of that? A pet is a big responsibility. Not a symbol of fiscal policy."

King Kong went back to the blue Gatorade in the kitchen.

Then he knocked over the trash can and started eating something—Clip's bills, it looked like. Everything the dog did now had much more meaning.

I could tell Clip was mad at me, so I walked two blocks to the bus stop—he wasn't going to give me a ride in the Aptitude. I waited for a minute and then remembered that I didn't have any cash. I started walking home. Clip sent me a series of text messages. "The dog is a metaphor," the first one read. I didn't respond. Three blocks later, he wrote, "Think about the best part of that movie."

I imagined the dog climbing the Empire State Building. Biplanes firing away. Spotlights. Clip screaming on the ground. Is this the image he wants? I never watched the remake.

Before I could write him again, he texted, "Julie coming over."

Julie was Ann Darrow—I Googled it—though which Julie I couldn't be sure. So this was a bad plan to get one of the Julies back. Clip was Denham. I got it. I didn't think Clip was "Untrustworthy" or "Insincere." He was my best friend. But I understood. He had chosen his metaphor and was running with it.

Back at my own apartment, I was still thinking about the economy because of Clip. I *was* broke. And now it seemed everyone was. Even Clip was worried. Was this a good thing? Probably not, but there was some comfort in no longer having to pretend I wasn't. To be rich, it seemed, was a sort of sin now. I Googled "economy" and started studying up.

Clip sent another text message. It said, "Julie here. Ooh la la. KK provided stimulus."

I wrote him back. "Does 'bailout' mean getting water out of a boat? Or ejecting from a plane? There's a difference." I waited and got no response.

I listened to a podcast about Ponzi schemes. The concept made sense to me, but it sounded like people thought it was illegal. I constantly made decisions assuming that the future would be better. Who didn't?

My vocabulary became richer over the next few days, and so I decided to play the market myself and call a Julie, hoping it would be the right one. I had consumer confidence. I was trying to do my part.

I invested wisely. Julie came over, and we stole a Netflix movie from my neighbors' mailbox—*The Secret Life of Bees*. We split a label-less bottle of something she called "Alien vs. Predator." The drink tasted like the Listerine that someone who had been drinking bourbon and smoking all night had spit out. It wasn't bad with a little ginger ale. Times were tough. This Julie worked as a dental assistant. She told me that many people were not going to the dentist anymore because they had lost their insurance. Some days she'd just sit in the complicated chair and read magazines and rinse.

When we went to bed, Julie asked if I wanted to put her bank through a stress test before I nationalized her. She thought that would be prudent. I had chosen the correct Julie.

The next morning I got a text message from Clip. It read, "KK missing. Julie, too. Hostile takeover."

My Julie was gone, too, but I was grateful. *The Secret Life of Bees* was still looping on the TV. I couldn't recall any of the film. Was that Queen Latifah? I stopped the disc and taped it back into its prepaid envelope. My front door was half open, but it didn't matter. It's not like I had a dog. When I was walking the movie back down to the mailboxes, Clip called me.

"I can't remember how the movie ends," he said. "Can you?"

I was confused. I said, "The Predators basically accept the

chick as an equal hunter of Aliens and leave." I was thinking of what Julie and I had been drinking.

"King Kong is an alien?" Clip said.

"Oh," I said. "Never mind."

"Julie went through my phone and read my text message that King Kong was a metaphor, I bet. She took him."

"That didn't take long," I said.

"For what?" Clip said. "Her to go through my phone? Or for me to lose the dog?"

"I'll be right over," I said.

I walked the twenty blocks to Clip's apartment, thinking about *The Secret Life of Bees*. My guess was that Queen Latifah was much too big to play a bee with a secret life, and she didn't even strike me as the beekeeper type, so I assumed the title was a metaphor. Maybe the movie suggested that we are all a lot like bees. Being unemployed, I imagined myself in new careers all the time, and bees have a job as soon as they are born. No application required. Maybe the movie was about the economy. I resolved to steal the movie again and also to Google it. Maybe make the movie *my* metaphor.

As I walked, I listened to a podcast called *Mark It to Market*. Made sense to me. I listened to a podcast called *The Toxic Asset Avenger*. It had been a while since I'd seen that movie. And I marveled at the pairing of those words, "toxic" and "asset." The things these people did with language.

When I finally knocked on Clip's door, I heard barking inside. That was a good sign. He opened the door with a sad sort of smile on his face. King Kong leapt and wagged. I was the second real person he had met outside of the cages, and he was glad to see me. I asked Clip how he was doing.

"Not good, boss," Clip said. "Look at what they did to King Kong."

When the dog settled down, I noticed blue spray paint on its flanks. On one side the paint read "Bad Dog." On the other it said "Go Home." Otherwise, the dog was unharmed. The smell of spray paint and dirty mutt was something, though.

"Who would do such a thing?" I said.

"'Untrustworthy'?" Clip said and gestured toward the Aptitude in the parking lot. "'Insincere'?"

"This message feels fundamentally different," I said. "This was not the Julies."

I said this knowing at least one of them was with me the night before. Could she have snuck out in the morning just to accomplish this? Were they still operating under the terms of their previous anti-Clip merger? Should I fess up?

"Want a drink?" Clip said. He pointed to a pitcher that was vaguely blue. I sniffed it, and it smelled like my prom in the late '90s. The economy blogs called that time the "dot-com bubble."

"It's CK Be," Clip said. "I found an old spray bottle in a drawer. It's cut with a good deal of blue Gatorade." He lifted his own glass. "It's not like I'm going to wear it."

I poured one. Times were tough.

"What's it called?" I said. "What do you call the drink?"

"It needs a name?" Clip said. "Old cologne and Gatorade?"

"Everything is something else these days," I said.

"How about 'Wall Street'?" Clip said. "Or 'Godzilla.' I don't care. I'm thirsty."

"To monsters," I said.

After we had finished the pitcher of Gatorade and cologne, scrubbed King Kong three times and shaved him, gone to the Coinstar to redeem our $16 in change, and purchased an actual bottle of gin, we convened the Julie-Gate Hearings. The Julies arrived about two hours late in a GM Compliance. It was a two-door SUV with a mirror for a trunk. It was bright red. Four Julies piled out. The problem had gotten bigger.

The Julies took seats at the air hockey table. I poured them each small glasses of blue Gatorade in silence, while King Kong moped around, thirsty and ashamed of his baldness.

My Julie from the night before looked at me as if I were a stranger. Had we not shared Alien vs. Predator? *The Secret Life of Bees*? The fourth Julie was their fat friend. While Clip and I prepared for the hearing in the powder room, he referred to her as "the pork," but I understood she was the boar meant to gore us.

Clip said, "They are going to argue for insolvency here, but it's really a crisis of liquidity." Then he grabbed at his lower back and grimaced.

These terms were familiar to me from my research, but I did not know what he meant, metaphorically. He could tell.

"They think," he said slowly, "I'm a bad boyfriend. But really I just don't have enough *time* for all of them at the moment. But I will."

Then he leaned against the bathroom wall and sank a bit. He closed his eyes. King Kong started spinning toilet paper off the roll with his gigantic paws. Clip took a pill from his pocket and crossed to the faucet. The dog had a drink from the toilet while we talked.

"I'm dying here, boss," Clip said. "I can't do it. It's too much."

"This crisis is all about confidence," I told him.

"I am a bad boyfriend," he said. "I'm a zombie bank." He swallowed the whole pill and turned gray.

"You are not a metaphor," I said. "You are a human being."

"I think I'm going to pass this kidney stone," he said. He had both hands on his back now and was wrenching in pain. "You've got to straighten this out for me. Go talk to them."

He put the seat down on the toilet, dropped his jeans, and sat down.

King Kong looked at me, and I could still see the remnants of blue paint on his skin. Clip was sweating and breathing heavy now.

"Okay," I said. "Let me know if you need something." I left Clip in the bathroom with his pain, and King Kong followed me out. The Julies were still sitting at the air hockey table, comparing text messages Clip had apparently sent them all, sipping their Gatorade. The fourth, mysterious Julie stared into her empty glass and snorted. I held up a finger to them, grabbed the gin by the neck, and went into the living room to review my own notes. My Julie—my secret bee—followed me.

"We were misled into a relationship we didn't understand," she said.

I took a swig. "Whose fault is that?"

"We are willing to accept some blame here," she said, taking the bottle from me and swigging it herself.

"What you did to the dog was a bit much, don't you think?" I said. "I thought we had a nice night together. You snuck out?"

"We did, you and I, have a good night," she said. A smile crossed her face, but she wouldn't share the bottle now. "But the dog is a metaphor."

I sighed. There was no denying it. I looked at King Kong—that climber of Empires—and he was shamelessly licking his privates.

When I was done negotiating with the Julies in the morning session, we had come to some concessions. The gin was gone, but the fat Julie produced from the SUV a bottle of something they called "Waiting to Exhale." It was a pinkish liquid with green leaves in the shape of little blades at the bottom of the bottle. It looked like poison sumac.

I shrugged and pointed to the bottle, "May I?" They conferred and stared at me suspiciously. "We're off the record right now," I said. "C'mon."

My Julie offered me the bottle. It smelled mostly like rubbing alcohol. Times were tough. As a sign of good faith, I drank right from the bottle without even wiping off the opening.

"There's fresh pomegranate juice in there," my Julie said. "And powdered Jell-O."

"It's delicious," I said as I put the bottle down. "Antioxidants," I said. "Is the movie as good?"

"You wouldn't get it," the fat Julie said. "Let's summarize what we've established and break for lunch."

In summary, we agreed that Clip had sold them on some options and futures that might have been questionable. I got them to assent that without a wedding ring, he was fully within his rights to do so—they were willing buyers. I agreed that Clip needed more regulation but asserted that we had to outline exactly what that might mean. We didn't want to limit him too much because it would stunt growth for the entire community, mainly me and King Kong but also some Julies.

The whole time, Clip was moaning in the bathroom, trying to pass that kidney stone. We broke for lunch.

Clip was sitting on the toilet, crying. "You didn't see me like this," he said. "Can I have some Gatorade?"

"Should we go to the hospital?" I said. "You were drinking cologne not that long ago. Your kidneys couldn't have liked that."

He pulled his jeans up to his knees. "How are the talks going? Where's the dog?"

"You could die," I said. "Kidney failure kills people. King Kong is right here." The dog was licking Clip's bare thigh at that very moment.

"What did you promise?" Clip said. His head was in his hands now.

"Not much," I said. "I admitted mistakes were made. They are willing to admit that, too."

"The fat one," Clip said between gritted teeth. "What is the fat one saying?"

"She's playing strong-silent," I said. "I don't think there's much substance there."

Clip laughed on the toilet. "There's plenty of substance to her. But I've never seen that girl in my life. What's her purpose?"

"She's a metaphor," I said. "For toughness. And for the larger community that your behavior is affecting."

"It's my fault their fat friend is tired of hearing the Julies complain about me?" Clip said. "Is it my fault she is unattractive? Where does it end?"

We agreed to try to end the afternoon session as quickly as possible. Did these girls not have some place to be? Didn't *they* have jobs? King Kong's tongue was blue from licking his itchy flank. The message was unclear now.

The Julies returned forty-five minutes later, each carrying a collectible, fluorescent daiquiri cup. There were seven of them now. They threw fast food trash into Clip's recycling bin. The fat Julie burped and did not excuse herself. The Julies I didn't recognize didn't introduce themselves. Some of them cracked ice from Clip's freezer.

"You went to the Recycled Bar and Grill," I said.

"Just for a minute," my Julie said. She grabbed me by the hips and smiled. She danced us to music that wasn't there.

"Clip needs a stay," I said. "He's in a lot of pain."

"We all are," she said. "Times are tough."

"No, I don't mean it metaphorically," I said. "He's leveraged."

My Julie scoffed; she didn't get it.

"So the whole world should stop, right? Because Clip doesn't feel well?"

The Julies all laughed. There was a general sputtering about the plight that is Clip-dating. I was overwhelmed and exhausted. Had he dated all seven? I walked toward the bathroom and looked at my phone. I had missed a call from a number I didn't recognize.

Through the door, I could hear Clip moaning more intensely now, and it sounded as though he was punching the wall. King Kong was whining along with him, licking his flanks raw. The Julies were laughing in the kitchen, spilling blue Gatorade all over the floor. Hopefully, the crisis was reaching its bottom.

I checked my messages. A recorded voice said the newspaper industry was a vital aspect of our society and therefore needed regulation. Did I have what it takes to help? They thought from my application that I did. I had an interview.

For a moment, I was relieved. Times were tough, but they would get better. I was on a new career path. Regulator.

But when one of the Julies turned on the air hockey table's fan, King Kong had had enough. It is an old, loud machine — a gift from Clip's father. The game required no real skill, just violence, just a franticness that feigned precision. Clip and I understood the game in an intimate way. That sort of banging away to score some small victory was familiar to us. It's a good game.

But King Kong began barking at the Julies in a dangerous way. He did not like their laughter at his master's expense, the way it echoed in the kitchen. He nipped the fat Julie's ankle, and she squealed. I halfheartedly called him back. His act was just a gesture, nothing more — a metaphor for his anger. Mine, too. He smelled it. But as the girls retreated out the door, King

Kong sat beside me, chest out, legs bowed, and he looked very much like a gorilla.

When Clip emerged from the bathroom, he wore only a T-shirt and his boxer shorts. His eyes were puffy from crying. We both said "Is it over?" at the same time.

King Kong rolled over onto his back, submitting to the day.

Clip knelt down gingerly and scratched the dog's stomach. "Did you bite one of those mean girls? Did you?"

"Not too hard," I said. "I think they got the point."

"If Julie-Gate has taught me anything, they'll be back," Clip said. "I created this monster. But I feel better. My stock is up."

I had a strange thought. I wanted to see that stone that had leveled Clip. I said as much.

"There's nothing to see," he said. "The doctor had said that might be the case."

"You didn't see it? So how do you know it's out?" I said, but it was a stupid question. Clip was pale and sweaty and shaking. There was a little blood on his hands.

"That kidney stone was not a metaphor," Clip said. "It's just a razor-sharp calcium deposit formed as a result of heredity and diet. If I'm lucky, it doesn't suggest a larger renal problem at work. Plus, it hurt like hell, and then it stopped."

It seemed Clip was already adopting a new language for this post-Julie-Gate age. Was he a doctor now, a scientist?

"And the dog?" I said. Had he given up on metaphor as well?

"I just wanted something trustworthy and sincere in my life," Clip said.

Then his phone began to vibrate and ring in a myriad of patterns and tunes. King Kong whined. It was clear who was calling.

"I have a job interview," I said, surprising myself. "In the newspaper industry." Even I was tired of talking about Clip.

"You see?" Clip said. "Recovery."

Dependents

J ANET HAD HAD THE baby six weeks earlier, and we felt ourselves getting a bit evaporated in Mommy-and-Daddyness. So when Memorial Day came around, we accepted an invitation to party. Truth be told, I had disappeared many months before, like a small moon eclipsed by the majestic planet of Janet's pregnant belly. I peeked occasionally from around that human globe, but really, I was gone. Even when people talked to me directly—pregnant Janet miles away—I was still nobody. I was, at best, a checklist: ticking down facts, purchases, and clichéd fears.

She had her moments of majestic beauty and great monstrosity during her pregnancy. She was back to beauty now, more and more each day. And I saw some stuff. The brutality of Pitocin and the nirvana of Stadol. A bloody little head where one had not been before. The glistening rainbow of the umbilical cord. When it was over, and he was breathing and screaming and pinking up, Janet said to me, "I've never done anything like that before."

But we were getting bored with our vibrating baby chair

and our swinging baby chair. Our Technicolor rattles. Our Diaper Genie had no more wishes for us. Our son, too, was bored. Even breastfeeding had lost its thrill; the experience was painful and unsatisfying for both him and Janet. He stared at us over his bottle of powdered formula, like, *Is this why you brought me here?* It was settled: we would leave the house.

We were invited to this particular barbeque because we had had a baby. Everyone there had. It was a new club we were joining, and their club seemed to work like this: discuss the kids for forty-five minutes; smoke a bowl on the back deck for fifteen. Kiss and hug the kids for half an hour, back deck for thirty more. Yell at the kids for fifteen. Light a joint in the next room. Eat a carrot; eat some celery.

We didn't do any of that. Janet and I sipped our beers out of cans in the living room, and the baby grunted in his car seat at our feet like, *Let's go! — Where we going? — Let's go!* Someone put *Finding Nemo* on the TV. The kids who could walk were climbing the bookshelves, falling off of coffee tables. They didn't care about the TV. Let me tell you about some of the people who were there.

There was one guy I recognized, Warren something. He used to run a record store in town that specialized in music people had never heard of. It closed pretty quick, in the space of a hot Philadelphia summer. This holiday afternoon, under his blanket of drugs, all he could mutter was, "Fucking iPod." He had a line across his eyeballs labeled "debt."

Another guy had the nickname of Clip. I didn't want to know the story behind that. *Finding Nemo* confused him; he truly did not know where Nemo was. He said interesting stuff like, "If I were an Indian, my name would be 'Bear Who Hates to Dance at Gunpoint,'" and, "Where the fuck are my smokes?" His own child was twelve or thirteen, which was old for this crowd, and the boy's name was Roger. Roger found a dark corner in the house and pounded text messages the whole time.

There was a bunch of other weed-head gorillas around, and I wanted to take a razor to all of their goofy, dirty hair. I didn't understand men who survived a Philadelphia summer with anything more than a crew cut. These guys with ponytails might as well be wearing powdered wigs. Plus they were barking through the movie, which was really the only redeeming thing here. My son, at six weeks, *he* wore a crew cut.

But one girl was in full-on mommy mode—no weed, no beer—just a constant mantra about her ugly two-year-old, Julian. I did not catch her name. But once, Julian called macaroni and cheese "Matches." Hardy-har. And once he crapped in the bathtub. I guess he thought it was a toilet. The kid said, "Blurt," and she said, "That's right, 'car.'" The kid farted, and she said, "That's right, Mommy has to go to the gastroenterologist tomorrow."

We young parents must think we are very important. All our kids have the names of kings and warriors and prophets. Everyone I know under five years old is named Julian, or Hector, or Ezekiel. What are we preparing them for? I met a kid the other day named Solomon, and he was on a leash in Walmart.

My own son is called John. There are lots of famous people with that name. The second president, the sixth, the tenth, the thirty-fifth. Then there's the famous bank robber. Many talented musicians. The recorder of the apocalypse, even. Janet named him for her father, a good man who died from cancer. But I think of him as John Smith, not the anonymous moniker but that captive of Indians, the lover of Pocahontas. I guess I was preparing him for something as well.

· · ·

Eventually, everyone left the room except for me and a guy draped like a blanket across the couch opposite me. Janet went onto the back deck to talk to the girls. My son was between my legs: in his car seat, going nowhere. We were still watching *Finding Nemo,* and it occurred to me that *Finding Nemo* must be an amazing movie to watch while on drugs. The colors and the dumb jokes. The deep feelings of loss. Fish. It was all there.

The blanket man sat up and scanned the room behind him. The two-year-olds were banging metal trains together, caboose into caboose, an improbable accident. Then he looked at me. He seemed surprised I was there, frightened even.

"I need to get out of here," he said.

I smiled and nodded. I thought he meant something like, *This is a radical party.*

He straightened up further, and I noticed he was in better shape than I would have guessed. His biceps bulged and tightened. Cords of muscle stood out in his neck. Short hair like it should be. His eyes, though, were as red as the wrong answers on a test.

"You don't understand," he said.

I didn't. I checked my son between my legs. He was awake but content, bobbing along the way he does. Living.

"Don't you have a ride?" I asked. That was stupid. Never ask someone on drugs if they need a ride. They always do.

"I was on leave from Fort Dix," he said. "I met these guys at a casino in Atlantic City. They got me stoned. We went for a ride. That was a week and a half ago."

I laughed because I thought it was supposed to be funny. He stared back at the door to the kitchen and then leaned in closer.

"They won't let me leave," he said. He was whispering now. "I've been kidnapped!"

I thought about the people who lived in this house, what

they might be capable of doing. I doubted they could keep a military man against his will. They were too fat. They were too friendly, too hairy. It takes focus to kidnap. Planning. Style. Doesn't it?

"I'm AWOL now," he said. "I'm screwed. But they drugged me."

I took a longer look at him. He was wearing a stained T-shirt that read, "I Busted Caesar's Slots." Then, cargo shorts, some flip-flops around his hairy feet. Standard fare. Nothing obviously military. No dog tags. No badass tattoos or scars.

"You seem perfectly willing," I said, trying not to sound like a narc. Fifteen minutes ago, I had watched him swallow what, in HIV circles, would have constituted a cocktail of pills.

"Oh, fuck," he said. "You're in on it." He slumped back onto the couch and put a pillow in front of his face. He actually screamed into it, very childish. My son just gazed, sucking on his pacifier. This guy was ruining the movie. Janet was still talking on the back deck. Nemo's dad was dodging sharks.

"What do you want me to do?" I said. I had an addict roommate in college who was always stumped by this question. It usually froze him in his paranoia.

"So, what, you're a narc?" he said. "You're a fed?"

"I live across the street," I said. "I'm no secret agent. We were just watching this movie. We've got to find Nemo. That's about it."

"I'm court-martialed," he said. "Great. You know, this isn't my fault. Jail. Wonderful."

"We all have to take responsibility for our actions," I said. My son looked up now and focused his eyes on me. Something he can't always do, mind you.

"This whole party seemed suspicious to me," he said. "What's it supposed to be for?"

Memorial Day commemorates U.S. soldiers who died while

in combat, I thought. Men and women of the armed services are supposed to be especially glad of this.

"Memorial Day," I said.

"Have you ever been to the desert, man?" he said. "Ever seen a bomb built inside a human skull?"

I said, "I teach English at the community college. I come home at night and watch the Food Network. I have a son. Don't put whatever this is on me."

Then he started with, "At night, in the desert, you can hear the souls of the—"

"Oh, Christ," I said. I got up. I picked up my beer and my baby and went to find Janet.

"Call the cops, friend," he said, now lying on his back on the couch, howling into the night like some submissive dog of the desert. "Call them. Tell them what's going on here, narc. Call your boys in. The choppers. The cuffs. Take me to Cuba."

On the TV, Nemo's dad and his friend Dory were bouncing through the jellyfish, trying not to get stung. Dory did get stung though, and kind of stoned herself. We have the movie at home and in widescreen. I've seen it a hundred times. Nemo basically finds himself.

Janet was posing on the back deck, inadvertently radiant in the sun, and got more so when I brought the baby outside. Golden arms on the railing. Frizzy hair from the heat. Her body still swollen a bit from the miracle.

"Baby boy," she squealed when we arrived.

"He's getting fussy," I said, which was not true. But we had this new way of talking to each other, describing our own states as if they were our son's. She understood. The kid was actually snoring to beat the band, to beat the druggy, party racket. We *were* secret agents in this respect; we spoke in code. I meant, *Let's go.*

We said our good-byes and marched back across the street. Our baby was enjoying the momentum in the car seat now, the wind in his ears. He stretched the new muscles in his neck and arms. He gurgled his pacifier out of his mouth, stoked as he was to leave that party.

Back in our own kitchen, we made grown-up drinks. The veggie platter had soured our stomachs, and it was getting late. Forget dinner. Our son oinked and mooed and quacked in his swinging chair. He would not sleep now. And he would not stop watching us.

I made a toast.

"I don't like those people," I said. "Or their kids."

"Be nice," she said.

We clinked our glasses and drank.

"Our child will not be like that," I said. I looked at our baby, and his eyes were crossed.

"Like what?" she said. "The parents or the kids?"

"Both," I said. "Neither."

"He'll be what he'll be. Himself," she said. She took a rag and wiped down the counter.

I had hurt her feelings because some of those people at the party were her friends.

"Clip was a nice guy," I said. In fact, at one point in the kitchen, Clip had said to me, "Cool baby."

She nodded as she took another drink. I liked her hair when it was ruined like this by the humidity. I liked that after the miracle she could share a drink with me, be stunning. I thought it was for the best that breastfeeding had failed.

"And the guy who ran the record store," I said. "I respect what he was trying to do. I bought a few discs there. Some concert tickets once."

"Stop," she said. "Eric was so cute."

"Yes," I said. "Eric was." I had no idea who that dude was. Another baby, I hoped, but his name—pretty normal—was suspicious.

"I'm glad we went," she said. She decided to cut up a lime for her drink. The baby was napping now in his chair, swinging east to west.

"The guy with all the muscles told me he was being held hostage," I said, casually. Just another detail from the party.

"What do you mean?" she said.

"He told me he met those guys in Atlantic City. They won't let him go home or back to base or whatever," I said. "He told me to call the cops."

"The baby is crying," she said. This was also true. He does this in split seconds. He is so genuine in his emotions; there is no lag time. His smile cracks on his face like an egg; then it's pure misery, pure tragedy. She left the kitchen for the living room, and then took him into the bedroom. I followed them, both our drinks in hand. She put him on our bed, on my pillow. I understood the gesture. She was mad with me.

"Should I call them?" I said.

"Who?" she said.

"The cops," I said. "About that guy."

"If the cops show up, they'll all go to jail," she said. "There's a lot of drugs in that house."

"You know those people better than me," I said, "Could they kidnap someone?"

"What would be the point?" she said. "They have plenty of friends."

"Ransom?" I said. "Maybe he does chores?"

"The most logical answer is that he was on drugs," she said. "The front door wasn't even locked."

I lay down on the bed next to my son. He was fascinated by the ceiling fan and told it to keep spinning in his own way. Or he was saying something else. Who could know?

"This is going to ruin my conscience tonight," I said. "That poor guy."

Janet took off her blouse and jeans and lay down on the other side of our baby so he couldn't roll off the bed. He kicked me in the ribs and drooled on her bare shoulder, but he wasn't going anywhere.

"There's worse things," she said. "Worry about how we're going to pay for our son to go to college. Worry about the destruction of the reef systems."

"If I were kidnapped, I'd want people to believe me," I said. "I'd sneak notes out of the house somehow. Do Morse code with a flashlight. He even knows Morse code—he's a military dude."

"Stop," she said. "Watch the baby. I'm going to run a bath."

She got up and strutted around the house in her underwear for a minute, looking for a towel and a book. She had a battle scar or two from the miracle, but otherwise—gorgeous. They talk about a glow that pregnant women have, and she had that for a bit, but now, it was sheer power that she exuded. What was there left to prove? A man would have to survive a plane crash to earn a swagger like that.

When she finally shut the door to the bathroom, I talked to my son a bit.

"That man was silly," I said. "He's not kidnapped. He's with his friends." I rubbed his stomach. "He's just with his friends and being silly."

He talked back, and the expressions on his face were so sincere. There was something he was trying to say. Could it only be *diaper,* or *food,* or *sleep?* I doubted it.

Janet came out of the bathroom. The steam and smell of soap made her a goddess from some enchanted lake. I told her as much. She fed the baby, I changed his diaper, and then we put him down in his cradle for the night.

We whispered a little in bed after we turned the lights off.

"Are you still worried about that guy?" Janet said. "The 'hostage.'"

"Nope," I said. "I haven't thought about him since we stopped talking about him. We've got our own problems. The coral reefs, for instance."

"The baby's eye is goopy," she said. "We should call the pediatrician."

"Okay," I said. "Let's do that. What do you want for dinner tomorrow?"

"Fish," she said. "Salmon. Or tuna. Something fish."

"We can do that," I said. "Nemo with lemon. Done."

Janet giggled. "You're terrible," she said. "That movie is cute."

Then the baby began to cry, and we froze. His voice, they said, was designed to make us anxious. I believed it. Janet got up and tried his pacifier. She tried rocking the cradle. She tried the fake little bubbling aquarium. He was screaming now. I took him to his vibrating seat. I took him to his swinging seat. He was angry. Little veins and muscles, little clenched fists. His face was as red as the wrong answers on a test.

We hadn't planned on having a baby, but here he was. He hadn't planned on us either.

And sometimes, babies are born too early and can't fight hard enough for life. And sometimes, they are snatched from grocery carts, or disappear in crowded malls, or even die, inexplicably, in their cribs. And sometimes fathers run. And sometimes, mothers say, *I can't do it. I've never done anything like this.*

I've thought about those things a lot.

Two hours later, our son was still screaming. Janet and I hovered above his swinging seat as he cried. It was two in the morning, and we could still hear the party going across the street. He swung to a calm finally, but John was trying to tell us something we didn't understand about history or the future, or something we didn't believe. We were exhausted, but we were still just saying in his ear, *You're ours, you're ours, you're ours.*

This Is Tomorrow

FIVE-YEAR-OLD TEE BALL WORKS like this: nine kids bat each half an inning. They are pitched three balls, and if they miss them, they finally hit off the tee. On defense, each kid is assigned a batter and chases down the ball wherever it is hit. There are two innings. Every game ends in a tie, 18–18. Every hit is fair; everyone is safe. Tonight, the weather forecast says some storms might be arriving, but we're trying to get the game in. We see the dark clouds on the horizon, but they are miles away. Plenty of time.

Defense is the real challenge. Many just play in the dirt on the pitcher's mound, with their gloves on their heads. Some turn their backs to the hitter just as they are about to swing. Some find crushed popcorn, or fire ant hills, or broken glass in the grass. Everyone eventually cries. Baseball is an impossible game of extreme focus and total boredom. But I wanted John to figure it out.

I'm standing between first and second, coaching the kids around the bases. Mr. Milk is pitching, and Mr. Warren is catching and trying to help the kids with their batting stance.

"Spread your legs," he tells them. "Shoulders back and up. Look at the pitcher." Little Julie looks good, her neon-pink batting helmet shading her eyes like a thug's. Julie's mother is in a folding chair behind the dugout, texting someone. I look at John. He's standing between second and third. He has his hands on his knees, watching the ball. A natural shortstop. I like it.

Milk is a terrible pitcher, but he's decided he's the leader of this team. We're too liberal to use the word "coach." His own son is in the bathroom, and seems to have a bout of diarrhea during every game. Is it a GI issue? Nerves? Embarrassment? I've been a parent long enough not to be interested in other people's kids. But there's no way the kids can hit Milk's pitches—they are too slow, too low. Julie whiffs at three and gets the tee.

John has yet to hit a ball pitched to him this season. In the tee, I see shame. No, a sort of corruption of the game. It turns baseball into middle-class golf.

Warren places the ball on the tee and sets Julie up to succeed. Good distance from the ball, good leverage with her legs, good balance in her tiny hips. She swings once, bangs the tee, and the ball drops. Warren jumps in, puts the ball back on the tee, and Julie swings too soon, hitting Warren in the jaw before he has time to get out of the way. The sound is nauseating, a meat-tenderizing noise. Warren stumbles off—"I'm all right, I'm all right"—but then he's spitting out teeth. Some molars, it looks like, and there's a lot of blood. At first, Warren plays tough guy. John gets very interested and walks toward home plate as Warren drops to his knees and then passes out.

Little Julie runs out into center field with her neon-pink aluminum bat. She's spinning and pointing the bat in the air. Her mother yells at her from behind the dugout while we check on Warren. He's conscious again but covered in sweat. Now he's vomiting. He's pissed his pants. Milk calls 911 as his kid emerges from the bathroom. John is just staring.

The clouds overhead are suddenly very dark. A cold wind whips through. There's a flash in center field and then a tremendous bang, like the loudest photograph ever taken. Julie drops in a puff of smoke. The neon-pink aluminum bat is now twenty feet from her. It's blackened and sizzling. She's been struck by lightning.

Milk and I rush out to her, leaving Warren on all fours, retching and groaning. When we reach her, her eyes are rolled back in her head. Her mother is shouting from her folding chair as if the girl is misbehaving. The ground beneath Julie is scorched black.

"Jesus," Milk says. "Can I touch her?"

I shrug and look back at John. He's standing exactly between Warren's prone form and Julie's. He seems conflicted about which violence is more interesting. He sits down and folds his legs. Crisscross applesauce, as they say at kindergarten.

Milk pokes Julie as if he might be shocked himself. He's wearing batting gloves. Nothing happens. He's a big guy and scoops her limp body up in the crook of one arm. Then the rain starts, and he runs toward home plate.

I jog to John, who has stood up but made no move to get out of the rain. I put my hand on his shoulder and push him toward the dugout. By the time we get there, the mothers have started screaming, but we can hear the approaching sirens. Warren is on his back in the grass with a bag of ice on his mouth. He was given this by some anonymous mother who placed it on his face, as if she were leaving a gift of appeasement for some extracurricular troll, and then took off running. Julie lies on the wooden bench in the dugout like a funeral for a young, shocked bride. She's breathing, but her hands are blistered and bleeding. She's also moaning, and her hair is floating in the air with a staticky life of its own. It's like some old painting of the apocalypse.

The rain increases into hail, and the noise on the metal roof of the dugout is deafening. More lightning. Red and blue lights are visible through the shear, but because of the fences around the fields, the ambulance has to take the long way around.

As quickly as the storm arrived, it is gone. Steam rises from the field. The wail of sirens has vanished, and John, buckled into his car seat, says, "Are we still getting a pizza?"

I call the order in, and they say, "Twenty minutes." I turn public radio on the car stereo as we wait in the parking lot.

This evening they are broadcasting a local show called *Worst Sex, Best Cigarette.* It's a call-in program where listeners volunteer stories. A month ago, the state legislature cut all funding for public radio, and it seems the producers have decided to give a final, artistic middle finger before the money runs out. Lately, we've been the recipients of all kinds of new rogue programming, including this show. Also, *Who Should We Nuke?,* a show that rarely talks about political realities; *W.Y.R.D.O.,* which stands for "Would You Rather Die, Or . . . ?," where the host creates elaborate negative scenarios and listeners vote for suicide or survival; and my guilty favorite, *Make Us Cry.* This is a collection of sad stories without the normal insight or upside that public radio was known for. Pancreatic cancer for people in their twenties. Brave dogs sacrificing themselves for children. Car accidents on prom nights, wedding nights, on the way to the hospital to deliver a baby.

Worst Sex, Best Cigarette is not appropriate for John to listen to, but he's not listening. He's paging through a book cataloging Lego toys, the majority of which he will never own. Lego Jamestown Disaster. Lego Roe v. Wade. Lego *Challenger* Space Shuttle. Most of the callers speak in euphemism about sex anyway, and they are mainly just unfulfilled by the act. The community is not rising to the occasion that public radio is offering them, and there's your reasoning for why the funding was cut. The hosts of the show offer no sex advice, but instead seem to be pushing the idea that all sex is unsatisfying.

The discussions of smoking are mainly about delicious meals once eaten, and the odd places smokers have been relegated to smoke since it has been all but totally criminalized.

John says, "Dad, Lego Lollapalooza. Look." It's a huge set—$400—not something I could afford. And he has no idea what Lollapalooza is, but it comes with a gigantic stage, twenty weirdo spectators, two vendor booths, and either Lego Jane's Addiction or Lego Foo Fighters. At home, I have a Lego Nissan Leaf that you can actually plug in. I was saving it for a special occasion, hidden in the closet, but now it seems pretty lame.

At seven p.m., the weather guy says, "High pressure is moving in place tomorrow like a motherfucker. It's going to be hot in this bitch once this crazy storm clears."

In the rearview, I watch John mouth the word "bitch" to himself.

Finally, the pizza is ready, and I take a peek at it in the car. For some reason, Pizza Pro thinks it is a good idea to put the pepperoni underneath the cheese, prohibiting it from becoming crispy. How dumb can you get?

"Did we win?" Janet asks, not looking up from her paperwork. She's wearing her dark-rimmed glasses that suggest seriousness, maybe even annoyance that we were home a little early. She's an economist working with a private firm that mines asteroids. I don't understand her work. She makes five times as much money as I do. I cook food for people at a restaurant owned by the company that owns pretty much everything.

"Julie hit Mr. Warren in the mouth with the bat, and he spit out his teeth, and then Julie got struck by lightning," John says. It feels like an accurate description of the evening.

Janet looks at me, and I just nod.

"They're not dead yet," John says. "Look."

He opens his hand to reveal two bloody teeth, their cracked roots mingled with grass trimmings and dirt. One has a silver nugget lodged in it.

Janet springs out of her chair and covers her mouth with her hand. "Where did you get those?"

I didn't see John pick them up, but there is no doubt where they came from.

"Give me those," I say. John drops them in my hand without a fuss, and they clink like dice. I wrap them in a paper towel and put them in my pocket. Warren probably doesn't have any use for these anymore, but I figure I'll hold on to them until I hear something. People make strange trophies out of things.

Janet is flustered. "Is everyone okay?" she says.

I drop onto the couch. John goes back to his room to take off his cleats.

"Julie was breathing when the ambulance arrived," I say. "Warren was, too. I got a pizza."

"Is John okay?" Janet says. There's no way to answer this question. He experienced no physical violence but witnessed it. He arrived home with teeth and a pizza. In fact, he seemed thrilled.

"This is not what baseball was supposed to be, if that is what you mean," I say.

Janet knows what I'm referring to. Two weeks ago a rabid pit bull was loose on the ball fields and had parents and players standing on the roofs of their cars in the parking lot. Eventually one of the coaches produced a gun from his truck and shot the beast. Play ball.

Last season, a sinkhole opened up during a game between first and second base, scaring the second baseman pretty good. He climbed safely out of the ditch, but didn't return to play this year. Our son saw all of this. He must think baseball is some sort of adventure. No wonder he can't keep his eye on the ball. I want with every part of my being for him to hit a ball that is pitched. Fuck that goddamn tee.

John eats three slices of pizza that night, drinks some chocolate milk, takes his vitamins, has a quick bath, and snuggles up in bed, happy and exhausted. Two people have nearly died at his baseball game, but there seems to be no residuals for him. It's just another day. While I don't wish lasting trauma for him, is it strange to say his acceptance of these events as normal is troublesome to me? A child without anxiety is . . . what?

The world used to make sense, or seem to. When I went to school, we occasionally had fire drills in case of an emergency, and while we kids loved the interruptions, the teachers always seemed irritated by this distraction—the clang of the bell, the goofiness that ensued—instead of focusing on the seriousness of surviving a crisis. Instead, John has classes whose subject matter *is* emergencies. His homework asks questions like, "If there is a shooter in the building, should you (A) hide, (B) run toward the nearest exit, (C) find a weapon of your own, or (D) none of the above." He circles D, and he's correct, apparently. But he can't say what his teacher had actually advised.

My guess is the lesson is to play dead. Imagine that. It's decent advice, but seems the opposite of education.

When we talk at bedtime, John speaks from a near dream state, and it is getting difficult to know what is real and what is just the play of his mind.

"We're going on a field trip Friday," he says.

"Oh, yeah?" I say. "Where to?"

"We're going to the zoo," he says. "To watch an exorcism."

"An exorcism, huh?" I say. "Is that the right word? I thought you went to the zoo to see animals."

"We're going to watch them take a demon out of a very bad giraffe," he says.

I go cold and speechless for a minute.

"Well, night-night," I say. "I love you."

This night was not a defining moment for John. His world simply works this way, no matter how much Janet and I have tried to inspire a more traditional version of normalcy. When he was two years old, he would not speak. We were given a questionnaire to fill out and they diagnosed him with autism. Then I took the test. I was autistic. So was Janet. So was everyone I knew.

At work the next morning, I cut into a tomato, and despite its deeply red skin, the flesh inside is white—pinkish, at best. I show it to the owner, Clip.

"This isn't a tomato," I say. "It's a red, fibrous bag of water. It tastes like my knife."

"I agree," Clip says. "But I get them from a distributor in a box labeled 'tomatoes.' What can I do? Get a new distributor? Grow them myself?"

Both seem like reasonable possibilities, but he doesn't see them that way. My own garden is dismal each year, and there's really only one company selling things these days. But I remember tomatoes. I remember pollinating bees, whole swarms of them. I remember baseball and zoos and romance. People seem to think the past is not worth anything, and it drives me crazy. I spent a lot of time there.

• • •

No one dies at John's next baseball game, but only four kids show up on our team, so we lose 18–8. We get a snow cone anyway, so it's all sunshine and butterflies. The news about Mr. Warren is positive, but he won't be back coaching until soccer in the fall. I play catcher instead, but keep my distance. Murkier news about Little Julie. Someone says "seizures." Someone says "superpowers." She's our neighbor two doors down.

When John and I come home with Chinese food, Janet is ashen among her glasses and paperwork. I set John up with some chicken fried rice, and Janet beckons me to the bedroom.

"How do you feel about 30 percent?" she says.

"It's a pretty good batting average," I say.

"I'm serious," she says.

"Do tell," I say.

The company she has been consulting for has discovered an asteroid with a 30 percent chance of hitting the Earth. A big one. No one is panicking yet. She's saying she shouldn't even be telling me, but how could she not, and 30 percent is pretty small, right? This is classified probably. I can't tell anyone. It's four miles across.

"Two years," she says.

"That's just great," I say, like the discovery of the event caused it. All of these people thinking about the future but not really doing anything about it.

"I'm sure they're telling people about this," she says. "There's experts working on it right now."

"You?" I say. I trust Janet. She could deflect it, couldn't she?

"We're mining a different asteroid," she says. "Telling the investors about this makes no sense. We're proceeding as planned. I signed a contract."

I sit on the bed and wipe my hands down my face. John comes in and asks if he can try chopsticks; he knows last time he just made a mess, but promises it will be different this time. I say, sure, fine, make the mess, who cares?

The doorbell rings at eight thirty, and it's my sister. Through the peephole it seems that she's carrying two rolling suitcases. I haven't seen her in months.

"Hey, little brother," she says when I undo all the elaborate locks on the door. "Everything's getting worse."

"Aunt Lovely!" John screams, launching from his bedroom, where we tell him to go if there is ever an unexpected knock on the door.

Lovely scoops him up with genuine affection. I find a bottle of pink wine in the garage, pour her a glass, and plop in a few ice cubes. I know the drill. Her luggage hovers by the front door. We're in for a speech. The sooner it starts, the sooner it ends.

"Roger left me," she says. "I can't stay in that house." She gulps the wine. "What am I? Some forgetful elephant?"

While I blow up the AeroBed, Lovely produces a Lego Rosa Parks Bus set. John squeals.

He has no idea who Rosa Parks is or why it is recommended that you glue her to her seat on the bus after you build it. He puts her in the back of the bus, and I say, "No, that's not the point," and my sister says, "Just let the kid play the way he wants."

Lovely has four more glasses of pink wine in a half hour and says, "I swear he's a werewolf. Every time the moon was full, he didn't come home at night. I'd find him groggy and naked on the couch the next morning. Explain that to me?"

"Uncle Roger is a werewolf?" John says. It's past his bedtime, but he's thrilled about this sort of access to adult conversation. He's nursing a blue Popsicle, perched on the arm of the sofa, loving the fact that he's been ignored for the last hour.

"No," I say. "Aunt Lovely is just upset."

"Not so upset to be inaccurate," she says. "He's not your uncle anymore. He's a monster."

John's eyes widen, but I scoop him up. "Bedtime, dude. Brush your teeth."

He stomps back to the bathroom, and I notice Janet lean in to the conversation with Lovely. I overhear some discussion of hair and nails.

This wolf talk is straight out of my mother's vocabulary before she was diagnosed and medicated. Mom talked a lot about the wolves that would steal our sheep. Of course we had no sheep in Philadelphia, and no one in our neighborhood even had a backyard, much less a dog. It frightens me Lovely is bringing this back up.

John is snuggled up and buzzing with excitement. I get it, but am feeling overwhelmed by bad news. I turn his lullaby music on, turn his fish tank light off, and hope to say something smart.

"I like when Aunt Lovely is here," he says.

"Me, too," I say.

"Is Uncle Roger really a werewolf?" he says.

"I doubt it," I say. "I think Aunt Lovely is just mad at him. And I don't think werewolves are real. They are just in stories."

He settles in and relaxes. I rub his body from neck to feet, thinking about the world he's inheriting until his breathing gets regular and until the conversation in the living room has ended.

When I come back out, Janet has gone back to our bedroom, but Lovely still wants to talk.

"He'll show up here tonight, you know?" she says. "The werewolf. He won't like what I've done."

I have a friendly history with Roger, but I recheck all the locks on the front door anyway. There are six. The back door has three. The windows are barred. The fence electrifies at eleven p.m.

"So, assuming you're right," I say, "why bring him here? I have a family, you know?"

"I just wanted to feel safe," she says.

On cue, something bangs against the front door. The steel reinforcement fights back. Now there is scraping—claws, it sounds like. I find John's baseball bat and twirl it.

"He can't get in," I say. "But what did you do to make him so angry?"

"I slept with his friends and spent a lot of his money and wrecked his car and slapped his mother," she says. "Okay?"

I walk to the back door and double-check the locks. I see a pair of yellow eyes flash in the backyard. A shadow leaps the fence. I think, *Fuck it.* I settle Lovely onto the AeroBed, and crawl in bed with Janet. John has been asleep for a few hours. I have a Desert Eagle in the drawer next to me. The most expensive gun I could buy.

When I get out of the shower the next morning, the whole family is laughing over French toast and fresh strawberries tossed with sugar. I'm astonished. Lovely hands me a cup of coffee, Janet smacks my butt through the towel, and John starts talking about the zoo field trip. The world is fine.

"We were thinking we should have a barbeque," Janet says. "Invite everyone over."

"Okay," I say. "That seems appropriate."

"Lighten up, little brother," Lovely says. "Let's celebrate something."

• • •

On my way to work, I turn on *Make Me Cry*. It's pancreatic can-cer again, but I'm starting to build up a tolerance. I'm basically dry, though it is not the caller's fault. I consider calling about werewolves and big sisters and killer asteroids, but don't. I sip my coffee instead. I sip the normalcy of the world I think still exists but probably doesn't.

In the kitchen at work, I crack eggs, and there are just yel-low yolks and whites—not demon chicks, not bloody mes-sages, not anything absurd. Clip arrives with a crate of expen-sive mushrooms, fresh baguettes, and Jersey tomatoes he stole out from under the buyers for the casinos in Atlantic City. He drags in two coolers of fresh meat. He went to an actual butcher.

"You were right," he says.

I cut into a tomato, and it is ugly and asymmetrical, but dammit, it tastes like a tomato. We high-five and rewrite the lunch menu.

"We're having a barbeque," I say. "You should come."

I leave work after the lunch rush. At the grocery store, I get three skirt steaks to marinate, tiger shrimp, fennel, endive, aru-gula, clementine oranges, radicchio, cantaloupe, prosciutto, honeydew, and two gallons of whole bean vanilla ice cream. Anything that's expensive I put into the cart because if I use my credit card, I can pay less for my gas. It's all the same com-pany—they are fine with my money in different ways.

At the beer distributor, I buy two sampler cases of a brand I've never touched. Summer Kiwi Wheat, Pig's Blood Red Lager, Chocolate Chip Stout, Carrot Ginger Pale Ale.

John returns from the exorcism at the zoo. On his report, some black winged creature flew from the giraffe's head after the priest did his ritual. Pure evil. John is telling the family what the power of Christ compels animals to do, but I'm chopping vegetables, so I'm okay to laugh about it. Using a knife has always been calming for me.

Clip arrives with four lobsters squirming in a bag. I get the water boiling and open a beer for him and pour it in a cold glass. The liquid is greenish. Clip stares at it for a moment, then shrugs and takes a big gulp.

"We had a good day, but the restaurant is doomed," he says. "I can't keep it going—we're hemorrhaging money. I'm sorry I'm saying this at your party, but I like you and your family. You should know, but don't tell anyone yet. It'll be a few more weeks."

"But all that good food today . . ." I say.

"Can't save the restaurant," he says. "Look. I'm out of a job, too. I went rogue with buying all that good food. But this ain't my decision." He points up. "An act of God or whatnot. The company."

I drop the lobsters in the pot, they squeal, and I open a beer that does not taste like beer for myself. Cheers.

Outside on the deck, everyone is happy. Lovely is sipping her pink wine. Janet has John on her lap, tickling him. Clip has emerged, telling restaurant horror stories for laughs. The chokers. The allergic. The steaks are searing; the shrimp are marinating. I go into the bathroom and cry for a minute.

Then there's a knock on the front door. It's Roger. He wears a neck brace and carries a bag of fresh corn.

"Not sure Lovely wants you here, man," I say.

"I heard there was a barbeque," he says. "I have some important things to tell her."

"Happy things, I hope," I say. "We're done with bad news around here."

He points to his brace and says, "Surely there's at least a
funny story here. C'mon, let me in."

John appears behind me, and Roger produces the Lego
CNN *Situation Room* set. It has tiny Wolf Blitzer and tiny Dr.
Sanjay Gupta figures and an interactive screen that wirelessly
connects to CNN.com. John has wanted this for a long time.
When he connects it to the wireless, it tells us we are on tor-
nado watch. He takes it to his room, fascinated.

I shuck the corn and pull the butter from the fridge to
soften. Roger opens a strange beer.

"I've always loved Lovely," he says. "You know that. Even
when she runs away. And she always does that. You know that.
She's your sister."

"She told us you were a werewolf," I said. "Why would I let
a werewolf in my house?"

"I'm a hairy, overheated man," Roger says. "Our air conditioner is shit, so if I come in late, I strip and sleep on the couch.
She's told you what *she's* done? You and I have been friends for
a long time."

The doorbell rings again. It's Mr. Warren and Mr. Milk.
Warren smiles through a wired jaw and two black eyes. He's
brought two bags of ice, which seems appropriate. Milk has a
bag full of romaine lettuce. When I let them in, they pull cans
of regular beer from their pockets. I hadn't invited them but
am glad to see them. Roger nods, and walks outside. They also
produce a Lego set for John—he comes out of his room just
long enough to snag it. It's Lego SETI. Two radio antennae
arrays that really work, really sort through SETI data, and a
tiny, wishful-thinking gray alien. John whoops and rips the box
open as he heads back to his room.

Tornadoes never happen in Philadelphia, so the barbeque
continues. On the deck, Roger puts his arm around Lovely's

waist. She laughs at his presence and bumps his hip, sips her pink wine. Janet is using her pointer fingers to describe something about her work. She's drawing shapes in the air, talking, I think, about triangulation with asteroids. Everyone smiles at her descriptions. Warren lounges in an Adirondack chair, holds a cold beer to his head, and angles a strawed beer toward his mouth. Milk puts the romaine lettuce on the top shelf of the hot grill and says, "Trust me. It's delicious." Clip looks at me and raises his eyebrows.

I turn on public radio in the kitchen, and the weatherman says, "There's a M-er F-ing tornado on the ground in Chester County. It's moving north-northeast, they say. If they hadn't unplugged our radar, I could say more. I'm just looking at the TV. See you in Oz, Philadelphia! This was special coverage from the station your government no longer pays for. What a world. What a world . . ." and he fades himself out. But before his mic goes quiet, I hear him say, "Look at that—" and then the programming returns to *Your Best Beatbox,* and I cut it off. It's basically people calling in to spit into their phones, the same skeletal song over and over.

I pull the lobsters out of the pot. I flip the steaks on the grill. I look at the sky. It's as green as a Christmas tree, but no one else seems to notice. I find room for the shrimp next to the steaks, and hand Clip a plate full of corncobs. "You can handle this, right?" He usually tells me how to cook, but this is my house, dammit, my restaurant.

I'm preparing the plate of melons and cured meat when my phone rings. It's my father.

"Greetings from the Tropical Fringe!" he says. He and Mom have been living in Tampa Bay for the last two years, imagining themselves as pioneers in their retirement.

"Hey, Dad," I say. "We're having a barbeque right now. What's up?"

"Well, the Weather Channel says there's a tornado heading your way," he says. "Apparently, you and Janet and John should be in your bathtub with a mattress covering you up. Helmets would be a good idea, too, they say. What are you doing even answering the phone?"

"Talking to you," I say. "There's like ten people here."

"Better get somewhere safe," Dad says. "With ten helmets. Mom wants to say something."

There's some ruckus; then my mother speaks quietly: "They say on the Weather Channel that Fox Chase is in the storm's path. Please be safe. We sent John a Lego set. Let us know when it gets there. It's Lego Roswell. Get in the bathtub." Then the line goes dead.

There's a gust of wind outside that makes everyone on the deck say, "Whoa!" It blows the flame on the grill out, but everything seems done, so we move the party inside, and I shut the propane tank off.

On the dining room table there is a platter of sliced flanked steak, grilled shrimp, four split lobster tails, cantaloupe and honeydew with prosciutto, a salad with mixed greens and oranges and fennel. Grilled corn and romaine. It's a feast. I make sure everyone has a drink, and turn the radio back on.

The host is now mimicking a civil defense siren. It's more alarming than the real thing. He's not speaking, just sort of howling into his microphone. Roger smiles at this. We all check our phones to see a big hook of reddish-purple on the radar heading our way.

It should be clear by now that I spend a lot of time trying to make everyone else happy. It's not clear to me what would make me feel that way. When John gets a new Lego set, I guess I share in some of that constructive joy. Janet's esoteric, scientific successes. But sometimes, it just seems everyone is so angry, and that makes me angry, but I have no solution to that.

We do have a hallway in this house, not exposed to windows, and it seems we should congregate there. The bathtub isn't an option for all of us. "We should get in the hallway," I say. "This storm."

Laughter. Roger's eyes flash yellow, and Clip puts some butter in the microwave for the lobster. Warren and Milk crack open new beers and stare at me.

"I mean it," I say. "A little girl got struck by lightning just last week. This isn't something to play around with. *Tornado warning.*"

Janet says, "Where's John?"

"This is Philadelphia," Clip says. Then the real civil defense sirens start. I had never heard them before, but it is clear they aren't announcing good news.

Janet says, "John? John!" and then the power goes out with a thump.

There's still a strange light from the window — purple now — so the party moves into the hallway. The wind is knocking on the windows with a big fist, and Janet and I find John in his bedroom, lording over his new Lego constructions like a demigod. She wraps him up in his comforter, pushes him into the center of everyone in the hallway, and sits on top of him like a hen. The rain starts battering the roof, then the hail again.

My phone rings and it's my parents.

"Put me on speaker," Dad says. "Your mother wants to hear that you're safe." John and Janet and Lovely are crying a little. Warren and Milk are daring each other to go outside to watch the storm approach. Clip and Roger are silent for once in this whole book.

"What's the Weather Channel saying?" I say. "Our power's out."

I hear my mother squeal; then Dad says, "You're in the bull's-eye. Tornado on the ground. A mile and a half across. Is that big?"

"Where's Lovely?" Mom says. I've heard this question before.

"She's here," I say, even as I watch her creeping toward the front door, fussing with all of the locks as if their tumblers might help.

The cliché is that tornadoes sound like approaching freight trains. It might be more accurate to say that freight trains have tried unsuccessfully to approximate the natural fury of tornadoes. The rumbling chaos builds; the house shakes and shakes until it seems it wouldn't be possible for it to keep standing. When the noise can't get more intense, must break for better or worse, it keeps pushing louder. We're all screaming, I think, but it's pointless. When I open my eyes, it's just everyone with their mouths open, no unique noise above the wrath of the storm. I shut my eyes again and clamp my dumb mouth shut.

I have my arms around Janet, who has her arms around John. I push my whole life into my spine, hoping I can brace whatever falls. The blare is so intense it's like a reverse sort of silence. But then there's an extra creak and snap above the din, and a whoosh, and a tree destroys our living room. I squeeze Janet and John tighter and wait for the next crushing blow.

The experts on TV have been talking for a while about the "new normal." Five-dollar gas and eight-dollar coffee. It feels like a sophisticated way of admitting defeat. How could something be both "new" and "normal"? How could tasteless produce, tornadoes in Philadelphia, tee ball sinkholes, possessed zoo animals, kids holding teeth, and every other horrid thing I've mentioned here be *normal?* There is no comfort in that phrase. Talking fancy about something doesn't explain it.

Still, there is some normalcy here. No doubt, these are my people, for better or worse. I'm not surprised to find myself trapped once again with them. Nothing new about that.

The wind is pushing our house over like we're little piggies and I think, *Wolves*. The wolves of the world have finally arrived.

After five minutes or so, the volume on the world abates. Dad, still on speakerphone, speaks first. He says, "Someone talk to me. Please."

I look for John, and he's huddled underneath his mother, half awake, barely aware of the terror in the nest Janet has made. She shifts and kisses his forehead. Roger is whispering in Lovely's ear, but she's still crying a little. Clip gives me a thumbs-up, then gives me the finger. Warren and Milk pull more regular beers out of their pockets and crack them open.

"We're all right, Dad," I say, and again Mom squeals in the background. "Let me call you back."

I open the door to the living room to see the small oak tree from the front yard lying across our couch. There's a cold mist and leaves blowing in from the hole in the roof and front wall, but it could be worse. The flat screen still hangs on the wall. The door with its six locks is still intact in its frame. The food on the dining room table is still steaming a bit. It's only been ten minutes since I put it there.

We creep out of the hallway. Warren and Milk edge toward the dining room, apparently ravenous because of the storm. They pick at the steak and the shrimp with guilty looks on their faces. Lovely and Roger are making out in the bathroom.

John is delighted by the destruction but unbalanced by his helmet. He hops on top of the dying oak tree and turns toward the TV out of habit. I pull out a few tactical LED flashlights from the closet, and hand him one. He shines it up. He's forgotten his Legos, has no interest in making some symbolic solution to this travesty.

I look up with him through the hole in the roof. This will not be fixed anytime soon. The storm is clearing, and stars are appearing. Rain is dripping from the jagged gap. If I had a telescope, I could maybe see that asteroid, but would I point it out to him? I think of Mom. They've stolen the sheep and left the wool. What sort of wolves are these?

Acknowledgments

This book would not have been possible without the support of:

The editors who took an interest in the individual stories: David Cameron, Jim Clark, Natalie Danford, Garrett Doherty, Ken Foster, Steve Gillies, Roland Goity, Robyn Jodlowski, Cal Morgan, Tony Perez, David Plick, Matt Salesses, Jane Smiley, Tonaya Thompson, Michelle Wildgen;

The mentors who were generous with their instruction and inspiration: Justin Cronin, Beth Ann Fennely, Tom Franklin, David Galef, Barry Hannah, Vincent Kling, Marc Moreau, Jacqueline Pastis, James Rahn, Brad Watson, Dan Williams;

The Gotham Writers' Workshop, which helped keep the lights on, especially Dana Miller, Joel Mellin, Alex Steele, and all the talented writers I've worked with over the years;

The Center for Writing and Rhetoric at the University of Mississippi;

The Mississippi Arts Commission, especially Diane Williams;

My Philadelphia Crew: Steve Haslam, Rick Mitchell, Phil Schorn, Will Seifert, Mike Walsh;

My Famous Times Writers at Ole Miss: Matt Brock, Will Gorham, Jake Rubin, Alex Taylor, Neal Walsh;

Renee Zuckerbrot and her staff, who were patient, insightful, and believed in the "Tom and Jerry" pitch for the project;

Carmen Johnson, who is keeping me honest, Mary Beth Constant for her precision, and Rachel Adam at Rodrigo Corral Studio for the great design;

The Mischkers, who have always treated me like family;

My big brother, Bill, who I am still trying to impress;

Mom and Dad, who drove me to the Greyhound bus station years ago against their better judgment;

Claire, my heart and doctor;

Liam, my master and apprentice.

© CLAIRE MISCHKER

Sean Ennis has been published in *Tin House*, the *Mississippi Review*, *Fifty-Two Stories*, the *Good Men Project*, the *Greensboro Review*, and *Best New American Voices*. A recipient of a Mississippi Arts Commission Literary Grant, he teaches at the University of Mississippi and the Gotham Writers' Workshop.